Highpockets

BOOKS BY

John R. Tunis

Published by William Morrow & Company
HIS ENEMY, HIS FRIEND 1967
SILENCE OVER DUNKERQUE 1962
SCHOOLBOY JOHNSON 1958
BUDDY AND THE OLD PRO 1955
GO, TEAM, GO! 1954
YOUNG RAZZLE 1949
HIGHPOCKETS 1948
THE KID COMES BACK 1946

Published by Harcourt, Brace & Company
A CITY FOR LINCOLN 1945
ROOKIE OF THE YEAR 1944
YEA! WILDCATS! 1944
KEYSTONE KIDS 1943
ALL-AMERICAN 1942
WORLD SERIES 1941
CHAMPION'S CHOICE 1940
THE KID FROM TOMKINSVILLE 1940
THE DUKE DECIDES 1939
IRON DUKE 1938

Highpockets

JOHN R. TUNIS

WILLIAM MORROW & CO., INC.
NEW YORK

PUBLISHER'S NOTE: On baseball teams before 1950, unlike those of today, it was not unusual for the team's manager to also play one of the positions in the field. In this book, Spike Russell is both the Dodgers' manager and its shortstop.

Highpockets

Chapter 1

"Him!" said the white-haired coach, scornfully. "That Highpockets! Wait till he learns to hit to left field; wait till he learns to play for the team. Then mebbe he'll be a ballplayer."

He raised one foot to the dugout steps, leaned on his knee, and peered out at the green turf spattered with athletes shagging long fly balls, at the quick, nervous movements of the infielders around the diamond.

"Him!" He yanked at the brim of his cap.

Charlie Draper, the third-base coach of the Dodgers, and Casey, the newspaperman, were talking in the coolness of the bench before the game. The sportswriter agreed cautiously with the coach. Jim Casey invariably seemed to agree, yet never did quite agree with the other fellow. This made for conversation and conversation often made for information.

"Yeah, I know, Chuck. Only he's liable to explode a ballgame any time he comes to bat."

The coach turned. "Lemme tell ya, Casey, that-there Spike Russell is the one who wins games. Know what Connie Mack usta say? 'A club can't win pennants without a top class shortstop.' He was dead right, too."

"I'll take Roy Tucker. That lad can catch three-base hits out there all day long. And at the plate he's the boy who comes through with the base knock that breaks up your ball game." Casey's deftness in keeping the conversational ball in play was unique. Somehow the other chap was usually doing the talking.

"Yep, he's murder. I check on that. But Russell, there's the guy who makes the big play that stops the other side cold."

This seemed to settle things. However, if Casey was a genius in the difficult art of listening, he also kept in mind the information he desired. "This new kid, though, what's the matter with him? Since I've been back he's been hitting the long ball consistently. He hits homers for you, doesn't he?"

"Look, Casey! You've been out, you been laid up with that operation—how long? Two, almost three months now. Right. I'll tell you what's the trouble with this youngster. You haven't seen enough of him. He's not a team player. He's not playing for the Dodgers. He's in there every minute playing for himself. Thinks of nothing but his batting average.

This has been going on all spring; everyone knows it; the whole club is on to him. So are the fans. You can't fool the fans, Casey . . ."

CLANG-CLANG-CLANG. The bell interrupted him and jarred the whole bench into action. Suddenly the cool dugout became a beehive of motion. The white-shirted players reached for their gloves, and the coach, uncoiling himself, went over to the bat-rack for his fungo stick. Casey rose and wandered across the field, pausing a minute first to talk with each pitcher in his warm-up. Then, turning, he came toward the stands.

"Attention, please. Line-up for today's game. For Brooklyn. Young, number thirty, first base. Tucker, number thirty-four, center field. Roth, number three, left field. McDade, number eight . . . right . . ."

A roar broke into the loudspeaker. Mingled in the cheers were other sounds, noises indigenous to ballparks, sounds that had in them derision and laughter and also cruelty and pain for those at whom they were directed.

Casey hesitated and glanced up, his ears attuned to the sounds and cries of sporting crowds. Stowell, the manager of the Braves, walked past and looked over significantly.

"They even give it to him up here in Boston," said the sportswriter.

"Oh, sure." The husky manager spoke over his

shoulder as he moved along. "They even give it to him up here."

Slowly the merciless cries died away. The loudspeaker could be heard once more. ". . . Number four, catcher. Russell, number seven, shortstop. Shiells, number eighteen, third base . . ."

Casey reached the stands. He opened the low gate that led from the field. Going through the rows of boxes he heard the comments of the occupants and, from higher up, the shouts of the mob heckling the right fielder of the Dodgers.

"You rockhead, McDade . . . you rockhead," someone shouted.

"Hey there, Highpockets, you bum! You bum, Highpockets!"

Even up here, thought the sportswriter. They even give it to him up here in Boston!

Casey reached the top of the stand and stopped a few minutes for a hot dog and a coffee. Down below, the game began and the visiting side went out in order. Then he climbed up to the press box above, just as the Dodgers were taking the field. His eye for news fell upon the tall kid trotting out to right, a glove under one armpit while he adjusted his sun glasses. Highpockets! Good name. The sort of tag Casey wished he himself had invented, like Bambino for the Babe, or Mugsy for John McGraw. Highpockets. The boy was tall, over six feet, with legs too long for his body. As he ambled out to the fence, his hip pockets seemed well up toward his shoulder blades. Big shoulders, too, for all his leanness. Casey observed his easy walk. There was co-ordination in his movements that bespoke the natural athlete and suggested speed—the stock in trade of the ballplayer, the asset that means an extra base on a deep drive, that turns the sinking liner into a put-out.

From the perch above, Casey watched the boy approach his position in the field. The jury box, the little separated stand of concrete in right field behind the visitors' bullpen, was crowded with youngsters. The kids rose, an agitated sea, when the Brooklyn fielder drew near.

Too far away to hear their comments, Casey knew perfectly well what they were saying. The boy moved toward them, turned to face the diamond, and stood pawing the ground, betraying his edgy nerves. The shrieks and taunts from the jury box increased, died away, and for no reason at all rose again.

Casey watched closely. Then there was silence as a Boston batter, swinging two clubs, stepped up to the plate. He slung the leaded bat back to the boy.

"King, number two, second base," said the loud-speaker above Casey's head.

The Brooklyn pitcher turned, leaned over, and fingered the rosin bag. The umpire adjusted his mask with one hand. The hitter thumped the plate. From the stands a horrible raw-throated voice that carried through the silence of the moment, penetrated the field.

"Hey, Highpockets, you bum! You bum, Highpockets . . ."

Why, even up here. They even give it to him up here in Boston.

Chapter 2

MOST ballparks surround themselves with the festering sores of a metropolis, slums or grim factories in the heart of a big city. Braves Field is on the banks of a river. From the press box atop the grandstand, Casey could see the green expanse below and, beyond the fence in center field, the blue stream sparkling in the summer sunshine. In the distance were the red and white towers of the University, and as he watched, a crew came down the Charles with a launch puffing at its side. Soon two more crews followed, winging their way through the calm water with another launch in attendance.

He sat quietly while the game progressed, listening to the chatter of the press box and the occasional remarks of the men around him. When the two teams exchanged places between innings, one reporter leaned back in his chair and asked, "This Highpockets, now, is he easy to talk to?"

"Not very. Guess he never was much conversationally, one of those mountain lads from some town in North Carolina with a name that sounds like a Grade B Western. Anyhow, seems he learned a lesson during the war. Highpockets was on some island out in the Pacific, and the boys in his outfit discovered he was in pro baseball, so they got to talking and asking him questions. One night after mess there was a gang sitting around chewing the fat, and he told 'em how he often nailed an ambitious runner off first. See now, a man singles, takes his turn around the bag, and starts halfway to second. Highpockets fields the ball leisurely, then suddenly turns and rifles it into first, nailing the runner getting back to base.

"Well, they listen, all 'cept one big soldier who gets up, stretches, and says, 'One of these days, young feller, that runner is going to bolt for second and you'll look mighty foolish.' Then he walks away, and Highpockets just sits there with his mouth open. 'Say! Who's that chap?' 'No one in particular,' they told him. 'Just a man by the name of Greenberg. Played a while with the Tigers,' says someone. Since then, they say he just won't open his trap."

"You can't blame him. Here he comes now. Let's see what he does this time."

The lanky boy stepped up, bat in hand, accompanied by a chorus from the stands. There were hoots, jeers, and other raucous sounds. The reason for this, the reason why the fans disliked him so intensely, was soon apparent.

The fielders shifted over to the right as he came to the plate. The shortstop took a position on the grass directly behind second, the second baseman went into short right between the bags, and the first sacker was deep and close to the foul line. Only the third baseman stayed in his normal spot.

The tall rookie swung a mean bat at the plate; his looseness was apparent as he watched the man in the box. The first ball he took. It was high, inside. The second was close also, and Casey saw from the press box that they were throwing onto his wrists, giving him little at which to hit. On the two and nothing pitch, he lashed out. The sound of his bat echoed all over the park. It was a sizzling ground ball directly at the first baseman's mitt. Ordinarily it would have been just inside the foul line and good for two bases at least, but not with the present setup. However, the ball was so hard hit that the fielder juggled it momentarily, picked it up, and then tore for the bag. It was a desperate race. Highpockets won by one step.

Turning, he walked slowly back to the bag. There he stood, waiting, watching the official scorer in the press box high above home plate. Thinking of his batting average, said the Boston players. Al-

ways thinking of his batting average, said his teammates on the bench. Look, he's thinking about his
batting average, said the fans in the bleachers.

Still he remained motionless, looking up. Then
the E sign to indicate an error and not a hit flashed
on the scoreboard, and the official scorer above
shook his head. The big chap on the bag flushed.
He clapped his thigh angrily and held his nose
with the thumb and forefinger of his left hand to
indicate what he thought of the decision. The gesture was plainly visible, lost to no one on the field
or in the stands. The hoots and jeers increased all
over the ballpark. It was easy enough for Casey
in the press box to understand why the fans were
down on him.

The game went along until the eighth inning
with no score on either side. Then, with two out,
the Braves filled the bags on an error, a base on
balls, and a bunt too hard to handle. There was a
long struggle over the next hitter, who fouled off
pitch after pitch to the screen. At last he caught
a fast-breaking curve and swung hard. The bat
on the ball had an ominous sound. It was tagged,
a terrific liner toward right that seemed to rise in
flight, that Bob Russell, the second baseman, leaped
for in a one-handed stab and missed. Highpockets
went back, his long legs covering the ground rapidly, back toward the fence in deep right, back until

he reached the cinder path just below the wall. Then, with no apparent effort whatever, he jumped gracefully at the exact moment. The whistling liner was in his glove.

Fast as ever, Roy Tucker was following the ball, too. He neared the fence, came closer as High-pockets grabbed it, and was only a dozen feet away. The big chap came down from his leap in the air, and with an effortless gesture tossed the ball underhand to his teammate. Then, turning, he loped toward the dugout. Even the jury box in right stood applauding as he came in toward the stands.

Casey noticed that the boy ran grimly into the dugout, refusing to tip his cap or make any conventional gesture to the yelling crowd above.

"Makes it all look so easy," said the reporter next to him.

"Just what I was thinking myself."

Now the Dodgers came in for their last raps, the two teams battling evenly and no one across for either side. Roy Tucker, the first batter, beat out an infield roller, and the next man, attempting to sacrifice, popped to the pitcher. There was one out as Highpockets came to the plate. The Boston infield shifted. A roar rose over the diamond.

The whole park stood. Out in left field even the two bullpen pitchers paused to watch the drama.

Every time he had come up, Highpockets had hit the ball straight at the fielders on the right side of the infield, going three for nothing. Yet the pitcher knew how dangerous he was and worked on him with care. It was pitcher's weather. The sun was low, and an east wind had come off the river, blowing the smoke from the locomotives in the Boston and Albany yards directly across the diamond. Out of the smog and smoke the fast-ball hurler of the Braves was not easy to sight. He had control, too, and could spot the ball where he wanted. The odds were against the batter.

Yet Highpockets seemed not to care. He stepped into the batter's box in a din of catcalls, croaks, hoots, and various forms of the raspberry, as calmly as though he were deaf. If he realized the importance of the moment or heard the derision of the stands all round, above, and behind, he gave no sign. Loose as ever, he stood swinging his bat, waiting coolly, while the runner danced off the bag at first.

The opening pitch was low, inside. He glanced over at Charlie Draper behind third. The coach rubbed his hands across the front of his shirt, and Highpockets tapped the plate twice with his bat to show he had the signal for the hit-and-run on the following ball. One glance at Roy Tucker off first proved that he, also, understood and was set to go. The pitcher wound up. Highpockets dug in his spikes.

He intended to hit, he fully meant to follow instructions, but the ball was inside, hard to reach, difficult to get a piece of, and suddenly he thought of his batting average and let it go past. Instead of swinging to protect his teammate scampering for second, instead of trying to foul the ball, he did nothing. The catcher rifled the ball down to second, and Tucker was out by a yard.

Of all this byplay the fans knew nothing. Only Highpockets' teammates on the bench, the coaches in the field, and Casey in the stands, who guessed by their movements what had happened, realized the sin he had committed. Roy Tucker picked himself up from the dirt and walked slowly back to the bench, looking intently at Highpockets in the batter's box. Highpockets, setting himself for the next pitch, never saw the look. Casey in the press box was much keener.

It was a fast ball, belt high, and he creamed it. You lost it momentarily in the haze over the park, and could only see the center and right fielders racing back, and Highpockets tearing around the bases with all stops out. Then you saw it, high above the layer of smoke and fog. The ball seemed to hang in the air, slowly clearing the bullpen in deep right and the jury box, which was a mass of excited kids with outstretched arms, and so over to the street beyond.

There was nothing grudging in the tribute of the crowd as Highpockets circled the bases. Yet the gesture he made to the applauding thousands as he trotted in toward the Brooklyn dugout could hardly be described as complimentary.

Chapter 3

LATE that afternoon he sat in the Coffee Shoppe of the hotel, his long limbs wrapped around the unsteady legs of the little table. Directly opposite was the door. Across the door was a thick, plush cord, and behind the cord was a line of would-be diners with hungry, anxious faces. Highpockets noticed neither the door nor the line. He was thinking whether to order another ice cream.

If he failed to see the waiting crowd, he also failed to notice the girls eating at various tables in the vicinity. Most of them observed Highpockets. His long frame, his face darkened by the sun of a dozen ballparks, his sport shirt open at the neck, made him noticeable among the white-faced people in the dining room. The girls glanced over at him from time to time, yet he never stared back because he never saw them. He was thinking intently about that ice cream. It had been a tough day, fighting the Braves pitcher and the hostile crowd; consequently he was both exhausted and hungry.

Maybe he should sort of celebrate that homer in the ninth with just one more shot of ice cream.

The waitress, a stout, motherly woman, stepped up and began to clear the table, which was piled with empty dishes. Her gestures were impatient and she looked over occasionally at the line in the doorway. To most people this would have indicated a desire for the table, not to Highpockets. Calmly he continued to concentrate upon that ice cream.

"Guess I'll have seconds on the ice cream."

The waitress, still looking at the door, spoke over his head in tired tones. "Hafta charge you extra for it."

With that enormous arm he reached suddenly across to the next table and snatched a menu. "Hit says . . . hit says . . . 'Price of ontray includes dessert.'"

The waitress glanced at the door and down at the tanned blond boy in the chair. "It don't include two ice creams."

He sat grasping the menu and thinking. Ice cream, thirty-five cents. That means seven ice creams in the drug store back home. Seven ice creams. In this man's town thirty-five cents for one serving. But then, it isn't every day a guy hits a homer off Jimmy (The Fox) Currier of the Braves.

"O.K. Gimme another, anyhow."

Twenty minutes later, the ice cream downed, he took the check from the waitress and wandered out and up to the lobby. The room was jammed with comings and goings, men with brief cases and women meeting friends near the big clock overhead. They looked at the tall, tanned youngster, and once in a while someone recognized him, looked twice as he walked past. But not often. He went across the lobby, past the newsstand where the evening newspapers containing the box scores for the day were headed: "Highpockets Homers In Ninth." At the far end there was a writing desk empty. Like the table and the chair in the Coffee Shoppe they were too small for him, and to make room he shoved the chair back, forcing his body to slump clumsily forward.

DEAR MA,

This took some time. Writing home was a grim affair. But he had promised her.

I'm doing fine. Hit a homer to win the game today in the ninth inning. That's my seventeenth so far this year. [There was a long wait before he collected himself and plunged again at the blank paper on the desk.] The clean shirts came this morning. They sure charge for laundry in this man's town.

Someone was standing over him.
"I'm Casey of the *Mail*."

"Yessuh, yes, Mr. Casey."

"I saw you were busy. Just wanted to ask a couple of questions. I'll wait until you finish."

For once he was happy to be interrupted by a sportswriter. "Nosuh. I'm just a-scribbling a letter to my old ma back home."

Casey could take a hint. He yanked up a near-by chair. "Home! Where's that?" Naturally he knew quite well; nevertheless it was a conversational opening.

"Bryson City, North Carolina."

"Bryson City, hey! What's the population of that city?"

"What's the what?"

"I say how big is it?"

"Yessuh. To tell you the fact, I don't rightly know for shore. See now, we live 'bout two miles from town, up Rabbit Creek a ways. I'd say, well, Bryson City, hits about sixteen hundred people. Maybe a few more."

"A small town with a big name. How large is your farm?"

"A hundred and fifty acres."

"Who takes care of it?"

"My paw. And the boys."

"You got brothers and sisters?"

"Yessuh. Three brothers and two sisters."

"You the eldest, hey?"

"Yessuh." He answered questions but volunteered little. The interview didn't appear to be getting ahead fast. Casey tried another line.

"Let's see now, you played baseball in high school, didn't you?"

"Yessuh."

"What position?"

"Well, I played sorta all over. Pitched a little, and played first and the outfield."

"Then you went west."

"Yessuh."

Casey still didn't seem to be getting much of anything. In desperation he asked: "Tell me about that bus accident. I'd like to get it straight from you."

"Ain't nothin' much to tell. I'm playing that summer for Boise in the Pioneer League. Most of the minors now, they travel by bus, and we're goin' over the mountains one day when we stop at a rest camp on the Pass. There's a phone message for me. Says I'm to come straight back to town and report to Fort Worth in the Texas League."

"Quite a jump from a Class C League," suggested the sportswriter.

"Yessuh." The boy accepted the suggestion but made no comment. "So I come back to town. The bus goes on, breaks an axle, slips over the side, and ten of the boys get themselves killed."

It was told casually and without emotion. Casey glanced at him. "Yep, that's how I heard it. You sure were lucky." There was a pause. "Tell me something. This hammering you're getting up here from the fans, does it bother you much?" He tried to ask the question indirectly, but somehow it sounded blunt and inquisitive.

The boy's look changed. His face was set and stubborn. Now he was out in the ballpark, slashing liners straight into the hands of the infielders in short right, the crowd jeering and booing and whistling as he trotted back to the bench.

There was weariness in his tone as he replied. "One team, one ballpark, they're all alike."

Something was behind this. Casey thought a minute. "Maybe you don't like Brooklyn," the sportswriter hazarded. He had no hope of getting a real answer, for he had put the same query to dozens of Dodgers before. No matter what their feelings, everyone always declared that he loved Brooklyn, the greatest balltown in the nation, and its fans, the finest . . .

"Nosuh. I don't like Brooklyn."

A Dodger who doesn't like Brooklyn! Casey was rocked. That's news! As a Brooklyn boy himself, he was slightly annoyed; as a sportswriter seeking a lead for his column, he was elated. He saw it in print: Dodger Home Run King Hates Brooklyn!

"See now, Mister, I'm here in Brooklyn to make as much money as I can. The seven thousand they pay me is peanuts to what the Giants would pay. Or the Cubs."

For once Casey was speechless. He mumbled. He groped for words. He had no comeback.

"Yeah . . . Yeah . . . I know, I 'preciate. But your first year up an' all that . . ."

"Yessuh, my first year up. I'll be better next year. This is my first crack at the majors. Only I've got seventeen homers to the fifteenth of June; that's better'n Ruth's record, better'n DiMag's. See now, next year I'm gonna get me a good contract. Real money, an' a clause like old Bobo Newsom had. His wife hasta go along on all road trips in a drawin' room, and suites at the hotels, too."

"Why, say, I didn't even know you were married, Highpockets."

"Nosuh. I ain't."

"Oh, I see. Got a girl, have you?"

"Nosuh. Leastways, not yet. I might have, though, by next spring."

Casey looked at him intently. Was this fresh busher taking him for a ride? No, he was serious. But a contract like Bobo Newsom's his second year in the majors! That's something!

"Look, McDade, be yourself. You're a rookie, you're just a freshman, not Bobo Newsom. Where'd you get those ideas from, anyhow? You have quite some ways to go, you know."

"Might be. But I'm a better player'n Ruth was his first season or Williams, either. No use kiddin', you know that; so does everyone. Mr. MacManus knows it too, and he's the boss; he writes the contracts. Next year I'll take care to get me a good one, you bet ya. Why not? I get on more than any ballplayer in this-here league. I've scored more runs, hit more homers, got more bases on balls . . ."

Casey interrupted the monologue. Apparently the boy could have kept on selling himself all night.

"Look here, Highpockets, why don't you quit thinking about your batting average and play for the team? Why don't you be a nice guy like the other boys on the club? Why don't you . . ."

"Yessuh. I know a lotta nice guys who don't win no ballgames. The nice guys are down in the minors; only the mean guys make it in the majors. See now, Mister, I'm just a-lookin' out fer me. That's all."

The sportswriter had often said the same thing about nice guys and the majors, and inasmuch as he had said it in print, he gulped and changed the subject.

"Kinda funny though, you never learned to hit to left field."

The boy picked him up almost immediately. "What's funny about it? I can hit to left. Only I cain't hit the long ball to left. I pull for the long ball." He hesitated a moment. "They brought me up here to play baseball. I do it the best I know how."

Casey attempted to backtrack. "Sure, sure, I know, I understand. Only a single at the right minute . . ."

"Yessuh." He had control of himself now. "In the majors they pay off on homers, not singles. You take the Babe, take DiMag, take Williams . . ."

Casey looked again at this character. A year ago he was in Mobile, two summers ago in Fort Worth, three years back he was playing for Boise, and four years ago he was pinning a photo of Jimmy (The Fox) Currier, the star hurler of the Braves, up in his room on the farm along Rabbit Creek. Now he was hitting a homer off the Fox to win the ballgame in the ninth inning. For a farm lad from North Carolina, he had his feet on the ground; he certainly knew his way around in the big time. It was true, as Casey had to admit, that in the majors they pay off on homers.

And yet . . . "Spike Russell's a great team man. You'll find he goes strong for team plays."

"Mister, look here. Spike Russell's a bad loser, like all major leaguers. He wants to win. I'd ruther play with a winner, 'cause winning teams pick up the dough."

This approach to the financial side of baseball was not new among ballplayers. It was, however, much more bluntly stated than usual. "Yeah . . . I know . . . sure. Only . . ."

"My old manager, George Hannigan in Boise, always usta tell me, 'You're only in the majors a short time, Cecil. Be sure and take yer pickings while you can.' See now, Mister, the club owners don't pay for co-operation and team play; they're payin' for homers. That's what brings the crowds."

After many years behind the scenes in sports, Casey felt he understood ballplayers. He knew the ones who were slaves to their nerves, the pitchers who never seemed to have it unless they were six runs ahead, who invariably got stomach cramps on the day the league leaders came to town. He knew the infielders who waved hello at the hard-hit liners in critical moments, and the hitters who tightened up at the plate whenever they faced the fireball hurler of the other side. He also knew the brash, cocky chaps, the boys with the easy dispositions, who were good and refused to deny it, who enjoyed batting in the clutch or coming onto the mound in the eighth with three aboard and the slugger stepping to the plate; the men whose ability blossomed under pressure, who always went for the stinging drive or the impossible double-play ball. Yes, Casey knew every type. Somehow this bird was new. He was a character all right.

Imagine a Dodger who doesn't like Brooklyn!

Quietly and with no warning, because that's how boys are when they want to be that way, the two men were surrounded. A sea of outstretched arms encircled the big chap at the desk, and half a dozen kids, pencil and paper in grimy paws, extended their hands. Without a word, he took their papers and wrote his name, carefully, slowly, and legibly:

Cecil McDade

Casey rose. "I'm much obliged. Thanks," he said. There was a column in this bird all right. His first name might be Cecil; but his last name was Tough-guy.

The big, long-boned youngster paused in the act of signing his name on a sheet of ruled paper that had evidently come from a pad at school. His tanned features came up slowly toward the sports-writer. There was politeness in his tone, and a kind of inner strength in the reserve with which he replied that impressed the sportswriter.

"Yessuh. You're shore welcome."

Chapter 4

WHEN a championship club slips in the early stages of a pennant race, its supporters make all kinds of allowances. They think of the run of injuries, the loss of a key man, or else they blame the weather in Florida during spring training, forgetting that the March weather in Florida is much the same for every club there. When, however, the team that won the flag the previous season is fighting to stay in fourth place in June, the fans are less indulgent. Sportswriters start speculating in print, the club doesn't draw so well, and the mob at home begins to grumble. Or they take it out on some particular player. Rarely do they go after an old favorite; usually they pick on a rookie and a newcomer to the ballpark. When the Dodgers returned home at the beginning of July, the wolves were on Highpockets with deep-throated yowls.

By this time, of course, Casey's famous story was a Flatbush legend. And all Flatbush was infuriated. "So he doesn't like Brooklyn, hey, the big bum!" "A Dodger who doesn't like Brooklyn. Whadda ya make of that?" "Who does he think he is, anyway?"

Casey had really let Highpockets have it in his column. I've seen bumptious ballplayers, he had said to himself; but this corn-fed takes the cake. He asked for it, so here goes. In a few days the story was a classic, known to every fan in the metropolis. Consequently they were on the rookie whenever he took his spot in the field.

They rose as he came chasing a foul fly up to the edge of the boxes. "Hey there, Highpockets, you squarehead."

"Yoo-hoo, Cecil," called someone in shrill tones. "Oh, Cecil . . ."

The lanky outfielder turned as he walked back to position. "Aw . . . act yer age," he growled.

Naturally the stands immediately responded, shrieking with vigor, delighted to have him answer back. Cries and catcalls rose over the sections in deep right.

"Hey, Rabbit Ears . . . oh, you Rabbit Ears," they shouted. Nearer the plate the fans stood stretching their necks and peering toward right to see the fun.

Spike Russell nervously pounded his glove as he watched the scene from his position at short. Shoot! Why on earth doesn't the big stiff keep his trap shut? Why doesn't he give the fans a brush-off? This sort of thing is exactly what they want; they love it when he comes back at them.

The heat was wicked in Flatbush, and it was a tough afternoon for the ballclub. Pittsburgh, in eighth place only because eighth was as low as you could get in the league standing, was on hand for a double-header. But the Pirates refused to roll over and play dead. Moreover, the Brooks helped them by not hitting. Highpockets went one for four at the plate, two of his drives going straight into the packed defense on the right side of the infield.

In the sixth, the Pirates loaded the bags with two away. Raz Nugent was called in to put out the fire, the third Brooklyn pitcher of the afternoon. He threw with care, but on the two and two pitch the batter got hold of a fat one and laced it hard to right. The runners were off with the sound of the bat; Highpockets was off, also. His long legs ate up the ground. He charged in toward the savage sinker that seemed a sure hit, while Roy Tucker ran over from center to back him up if the ball got through.

Highpockets, racing in, lurched forward, made an impossible stab, got the ball, and rolled forward, head over heels. To make it look even harder, he did an extra turn, and came up with the ball in his glove, one arm extended high in the air.

Maybe it was that extra somersault, perhaps it was the ball in his outstretched glove, the little touch of bravado, which so annoyed Spike standing anxiously near second as the runners whipped past the bag.

Hang it all, why can't the kid play ball like the others? Why can't he catch it and let it go at that! He's good, sure he's good; why does he have to advertise it? Why does he have to tell everyone how good he is?

The Dodgers scurried in to the dugout. Highpockets was the recipient of furious applause from the crowd, applause that he refused to acknowledge. Instead of touching the brim of his cap to the cheering fans, he ignored them as he came in and slouched down on the bench.

There, he thought. I've shown those rats in the bleachers. Let 'em take it and like it.

This was the play of the afternoon. Unfortunately the play of the afternoon merely managed to postpone the end. In the ninth one of the Pirates got a base on balls, and came across with the winning run on a double off the right field concrete. A scratch hit with two men down gave the Dodgers a life in their last raps, and then Highpockets came to the plate in a tremendous roar. It echoed and re-echoed across the field, for a hit would keep the rally alive, a long ball would tie the score, and one of his tremendous clouts over the fence would win the game. The count went to three and two. In a torrent of noise over the park, Highpockets whiffed on the next pitch through the heart of the platter, swinging round viciously and almost tumbling into the dirt.

A grim and disconsolate bunch of players trooped into the showers. They were in fifth place for the first time that season. The nightcap that followed was another dizzy affair. Each team scored a couple of runs in the early innings. Pittsburgh went ahead, 3-2, and the Dodgers tied the count in the eighth. The Pirates worked a run over with a snappy double steal in their half of the ninth, so again Brooklyn came to bat one run behind in their last raps.

Lester Young began the inning and the crowd excitement with a grasscutter between third and short. On the bench they watched as Roy Tucker struck a slow roller on the hit-and-run. The Pirate shortstop came charging in, saw he was too late for the force play at second, and nipped Roy by a step at first. One down, a man on second, and still a run to the bad.

Paul Roth hit the first pitch hard but straight at the center fielder for the second out. Then Highpockets, waving two bats, swung up to the plate. The stands were on their feet shrieking now; you could distinguish the shrill cries of the wolves, and the deep-throated appeals for a hit as he stepped into the box. The infield shifted to right, while the tall boy stood waving his bat significantly. Now the Pirates were packed close, blocking off his favorite hitting zone to right, with only the third baseman guarding the left side of the diamond. And the Dodgers in fifth place, below the .500 mark for the first time that year.

Everyone knew it was the big moment of the day, the moment all of them had come for. Not a fan moved toward the exits. They were watching the cool pitcher in the box, oblivious to the dancing runner behind him on second base and the menacing bat at the plate. Highpockets had been up eight times in all that afternoon, had struck out in the crisis of the first game, and only had a scratch single to show for the day's efforts. But he was still dangerous and the Pirates wanted that last put-out badly.

One after another, the first three pitches were low and outside the strike zone. The crowd howled with gusto as the figure 3 went up on the scoreboard in right. Three and nothing. Highpockets glanced over at Charlie Draper back of third, dug in his spikes, and set himself. It was a very fast pitch, up on his letters, right across the word DODGERS on his chest. With those keen eyes he saw it was good, took a vicious swing, and smacked the ball with all his strength.

Up it went, up, up against the deep, blue sky, far out to right field. There were the Pittsburgh gardeners standing with hands on hips, heads back, as it sailed over the screen above.

So to the dressing room, the Dodgers still in fifth place by an eyelash. The club had pulled out of a bad spot at the last second, and saved a game apparently beyond saving. Over in the Pirate clubhouse, the unfortunate pitcher sat with his shirt off, moaning. "Why did I do it? Boy, that guy takes his cut every time. He'll cross you the moment you take any liberties with him. Say, I'd give anything to be able to throw that one again." He slung his glove against the wire netting over his locker. "Shoot! I'd like to be able to throw that last pitch again!"

They were disappointed, yet the victors were far from jubilant. Was it, thought Spike, watching from the manager's room, the club or one man who had pulled out the second game? He noticed no lightness on their faces as they poured past his door, and little response to the big fellow's winning homer. Only one or two addressed him casually as they trooped inside.

"Nice work there, Highpockets."

"Great stuff, kid, that's really hittin'."

Yet nobody slapped him on the back, no one called him affectionately by his first name. There was no mirth or horseplay, no yapping or yelling as they shook off their wet clothes and showered in silence. They weren't free and loose as a bunch of champions should be. When a team is a team you feel it most not on the field but in the atmosphere of the clubhouse. That afternoon no one smacked his neighbor in the showers with the end of a wet towel or shouted insults across the room or yelled at old Chiselbeak, the trunk herdsman, as they dressed. Even the imperceptive ones knew things were not going as they should, and every player realized that they had been fortunate to break even on the day's play.

Reporters surrounded Highpockets as he yanked off his trousers before his locker. Did he know what the count was when he hit the three and nothing pitch?

"Yessuh," he replied slowly. "I thought he'd pitch to me, 'cause effen he walks me, he puts the winning run on first. Nosuh . . . what kind of a ball? A fast ball, right up here . . . chest high.

"Yessuh," he said in his slow drawl. "I made up my mind if it was in there to give it everything I had. When I saw that-there fast ball, I swung my hardest. How's that? Well, Mister, his fast ball does bother me, it bothers me a lot, it has something

extry on it, seems, like Mike Hammers, like Bus-
man's. Only when you catch it right, it shore goes
a mile.

"Yessuh." The boys stood around, writing on the
backs of envelopes or on folded copy paper. Highpockets slipped on his jacket over his sport shirt
open at the neck. He walked across the room and
took his money and watch from Chiselbeak.

"Thank you," he said politely to the old man.
He went over to the door, the reporters watching.
Nobody mentioned his game-winning homer, nobody called good night or asked if he wanted to
go to a movie or where he intended to eat. The
silence was noisy as he opened the door and stepped
outside.

All the time Spike Russell sat there taking it all
in. No use talking, this team isn't clicking, thought
the young manager of the Dodgers.

Chapter 5

THE youngsters on the squad, coming back to the dugout for a bat or to get a drink of water, glanced over at the strange figure on the bench with considerable interest. So that's him! That's what an old ballplayer looks like!

His lanky frame was covered with an aged piece of sacking which once had been a suit of clothes and now hung in folds from his shoulders. Years before, those shoulders had been the most powerful pitching shoulders in the National League; that afternoon they seemed shrunken and feeble. The Dodgers were playing in St. Louis, and old Mac Sweeny, the star hurler of the late twenties, had come in to see a game and his former club in action, from his home in a small Missouri town. Except to Chiselbeak, who had been around ever since the veteran sportswriters could recall, Mac was a stranger, a legend, a name only, Big Mac who had won twenty-five games with the Brooks his second year in the majors.

41

"Hey there, Mac, glad to see you."

"Why, Casey! Well, Jim boy, this is like old times. How are ya?"

While they exchanged remarks and reminiscences about former players and older days, out on the field the rival teams were in their usual pre-game practice, one group chasing fungos, another at the batting cage taking their raps.

"Which is this McDade? That's the lad I come to see, Jim."

"McDade? The big cub at bat, the boy slashing those deep drives to right."

"Him! Why say, I saw him in the basement of the hotel last night. Never knowed who he was. He hung round playin' ping-pong. Ping-pong! When we was in there, we didn't nobody waste time playin' ping-pong. No siree! And we had a right fielder could hit to all fields, too. Butch Kelly. This rookie, he said nothing, just played ping-pong."

"Yeah, he's very quiet. Doesn't get around much or make friends easy. Seems he sends his money back home, somewhere down in North Carolina."

The old-timer grunted in disgust. "Nowadays ballplayers save their money! We usta be interested in learning to hit to all fields; nowadays all these kids talk about is their annuities. Annuities, shoot!" There was scorn in his tones. "I recall the year I come up with the Cubs, year we won the pennant in Chicago. After the Series, I sat in a room in the Stevens with Jake and Red and the boys, and you know, Jim, when I got up after eighteen hours playin' poker, I'd dropped my whole Series cut. Yessir, over four thousand bucks. Why, nowadays you couldn't get a game of checkers outa these kids after ten o'clock at night. Nosir."

The contempt in his voice was majestic. However, it was lost on the little group of reporters watching the best infield in baseball dance about the diamond, cutting off hits and making splashy double-plays. At this point Highpockets returned to the bench for his glove, looking at the old player with attention, observing his shabby clothes, his forlorn appearance.

"Say, Mac," said one sportswriter, "see that stop Spike Russell made then? He's still about the best shortstop in baseball for my money. Even if the team *is* in fifth place."

"Uhuh," agreed Casey. "He sure is. He knows how to play every hitter and what to do with the ball when he gets it. You never see Spike Russell chucking to the wrong base, never."

The old man took a bite from a slightly desiccated plug of tobacco and shoved the remnants back in his hip pocket. Highpockets noticed as he did so the worn lining of his coat.

"Yeah, yeah, mebbe so," he said. "Mebbe he's a

Fancy Dan around short. Only he still ain't what I'm used to. You shoulda seen the Gas House Gang in my day—Pepper and Wildcat and the Moose ridin' in with their spikes high, crowdin' up against every ump in the business, jumpin' into the bleachers to haul out some guy who'd been ridin' 'em extry hard. Nowadays . . . why these youngsters, they tell me they'll take anything."

Highpockets winced. He's referring to me. The feeling didn't last. Thank Heaven, he thought, that's not McDade in twenty years. I've saved my money, I've got the mortgage paid off, and the farm waiting for me when I have to quit baseball.

Then the bell clanged, the old-timer rose, shook hands all round, and limped away. Highpockets watched the gaunt frame in the shiny suit. He shook his head in relief. That's not me in twenty years, no *sir*.

One hour and thirty-seven minutes later, five of the Dodgers sat around in the high-ceilinged clubhouse: Raz, the starting pitcher, who took an early bath; Alan Whitehouse, who pinch hit for him in the fifth and was relieved; Jocko Klein, whose finger had been damaged by a foul tip; Jerry, who had relieved Razzle; and Paul Roth, who had been taken out for Swanny in the eighth. Jocko sat on the edge of the rubdown table while the Doc worked on his finger deftly and expeditiously. Overhead the radio blared out the bad news.

"I shoulda stood in bed." Raz was disgusted and showed it.

"Me, too," said Jerry Fielding. "I shoulda stood in that bullpen out there. I didn't have my control. I threw to the batter's strength. Somehow I couldn't get the ball in there. I just didn't have it today."

"Nor I. Shoot! Some days you wake up with a headache, and you keep your neck out the window all morning hoping it'll rain, or you've been in an upper and ain't slept all night and you're stiff and lame all over, and you go in there and pitch one-hit ball."

"Right, that's it. Next week you feel like six million dollars and you step in and they belt the ears offa you."

"I don't want to be in no more pennant races. This is getting me down; it beats your brains out."

"You're not in no pennant race, Razzle. You're in fifth place. Hear that," said Al from across the room.

"Boy, ain't it a fact! Listen to them wolves out there."

The crowd roar rose, fell, and suddenly above the sounds a shriek penetrated the room.

"You bum! Oh, you big bum. Highpockets, you bum, you . . ."

"They sure love that tall guy, don't they?" Razzle rose and went over to the water-cooler while the chatter from the radio filled the sullen silences of the half empty clubhouse. "Well, they almost hand-cuffed him out there today."

"Might just as well have. Hits is all that guy cares about. His batting average, his batting average, his batting average. Shoot!"

"Yep, he's sure a loner. I wish they'd trade the guy. Mebbe we could have a team here then."

"I'll tell ya what I wish," interjected Razzle. "I wish Swanny's dogs would hold up. He can hit to left, Swanny can."

"Sure. He's a team player, Swanny is."

"Highpockets better learn to hit to left, he better had, that's all," remarked Jerry, hauling on his pants. "He better had."

There was the sudden crack of a bat over the radio; then stillness and finally that full-throated roar. In a minute the team came tramping in, first one, then another, three or four in a group, at last the entire disappointed, sweating mob. The pitchers threw their gloves against the lockers or tossed them to the floor in disgust, sat down, and began untieing their shoes.

"Shucks!" said Bones Hathaway. "Shucks, I had that game in my pocket."

No one said much. There wasn't a whole lot to

say. Over in the manager's room, Spike Russell sat in silent misery on a wooden chair, leaning over, his head in his hands. The coaches clattered in and removed their clothes without a word.

"Never saw the like of it, never," said the manager to no one in particular. He slashed savagely at a near-by chair, and it fell with a bang and a crash to the floor. Nobody looked up or paid any attention to the noise.

"They just don't think. Three to nothing going into the fourth, and they blow that lead."

In the larger room the players sat quietly, not talking, trying hard not to look at one another. From time to time someone peeled down to his socks and went across to the rubbing table. Spike leaned over, untied his shoes, pulled them off, and hurled them against the opposite wall. He shook his head. He was punchdrunk with defeat, with unexpected disaster, with problem after problem to which he had no answer: Swanny's age and his tiring legs; Raz's equally aging arm; Jerry Fielding's wild streak; Paul Roth's slump in left field. And Highpockets, of course; yes, Highpockets, too.

He's gotta learn to hit to left, that's all, Spike thought. He's gotta learn to play for the team. Or else . . .

Chapter 6

"WELL, we could always throw old Swanny back in there, Spike."

"Nope, not yet. Not right now; it's much too far from the end of the season. Swanny's dogs wouldn't take it."

"We'll hafta, unless this boy learns to hit to left field."

"He's gotta do a lot more than that. He's gotta stop playing to the crowd, and quit thinking about his batting average. He's gotta begin playing for the team for a change."

"Yep, he's gotta change. Somehow he must learn to hit to the opposite field," agreed Red Cassidy, the first-base coach. They were giving the club a going-over late that afternoon when the dressing room had emptied of players. "No use talking, he's gotta learn to play for the team. That means learning somehow to hit to the other field. Remember now, when I was coaching with the Reds before the war, long 'fore you come up, Spike, we had

Kenny Cotter as a freshman. Kenny always usta pull that ball to left, and I kept a-tellin' him he'd have to learn to hit behind the runner and shoot for those open spaces in right.

"Well, sir, seems like he never *would* get it. Next season the Reds they gave up and traded him to the Giants just on account of that one failing. We're playing the Giants at home, and they have men on first and second with Kenny up. So I swing our defense over to left and what's he do? He whistles the first pitch to right for two bases, scoring both runners. Minute later he comes home and calls over to me, 'See, Red, I can do it now.' Darned if he can't, too, and, what's more, he's been doing it ever since."

That evening after dinner Spike went hunting Highpockets through the lobby of the hotel. Unlike some men on the club who never missed an evening at the movies, or spent their spare time playing cards, the rookie was fascinated by city crowds, and was invariably to be found in the lobby of the hotel in which they were staying. New York was his favorite spot. There they mostly lived in a luxurious palace whose lobby seemed to be the crossroads of the world, a traffic station for the entire Broadway mob. Crowds swarmed around throughout the late afternoon and evening, holding his curious gaze hour after hour. He was excited and interested by the throngs who poured past, by the bellboys paging visitors, the continual stream of men and women coming and going. His eyes missed nothing as he sat with a newspaper in his lap, silently watching.

That night he was inconspicuous in a chair beside a pillar, half hidden behind a late edition yet able to take in the entire scene. Spike beckoned to him, the lanky boy uncurled his legs, and together they took the elevator to the manager's suite on the eighteenth floor. Far below, the lights were strung out in the evening haze up and down the heated city, and the roar of traffic penetrated the sitting room, which was hot after the air-conditioned lobby.

Spike came directly to the point. "It's your attitude, kid. Frankly, you aren't a team player. You're in there for yourself on every play. You can't seem to forget your batting average. This'll have to change."

"My attitude, hey? What's that? My hittin's O.K., ain't it? How many guys in the majors made twenty homers so far this year?" replied the big chap, his long legs sprawled out as he lounged in the armchair.

Spike glanced up. He started to reply sharply, checked himself, and looked at his visitor. The boy's face was frank and friendly; apparently he meant no offense. So the manager bit his lip, waited a minute, and then said: " 'S I told you last spring, we're always looking for team players on this club, Highpockets. Now I feel sure if we can only stay close for another month, the others better watch out; we'll be in there at the finish. But we won't stay close unless we're a team. You're a good hitter and can be a better one. Your future is in your own hands. If only you'd play for the club and quit leveling at those right field fences."

"Yessuh." There was a silence in the room. Then: "They pay off on the long ball in the majors, Skip. Twenty homers . . ."

The youngster's obstinacy annoyed Spike. Perhaps what also annoyed him was the fact that the kid had some truth in his remark. Yet his quiet assurance was difficult to take.

"Look, Highpockets, I *know* you can hit the long ball. I know you've saved games this year with those clouts of yours. I admit it. That isn't the point. Point is you aren't measuring up to what we'd hoped, you aren't a team player. And what's more, the pitchers are catching you off balance; they're throwing close to you and crossing you up with that pay-off ball. If only you'd stop trying to slug it. If only you'd stop aiming for those open spaces."

"Yessuh. Yes, Skipper. I'm well past .300 and I've had thirty-seven bases on balls so far this season."

He almost seemed not to hear what the manager was saying.

"And you've struck out how many times?"

"That's correct, Skip, I've struck out a lot. The boy who goes for the long ball always strikes out a lot."

"Once again, that is not the point. This club is a team club and you won't play for the team. Get it? You still can't hit to left field or you won't try. You must. Now see here, I'm giving you this chance but it's your last chance. Yes, sir, by gorry, it's the last. One more chance to learn, that's all. Otherwise back you go."

The traffic roar sounded from below, suddenly louder within the room. Neither man spoke for a few seconds, and this was the first time Spike Russell had ever seen Highpockets' composure ruffled off the field.

"You mean . . . the minors?"

The truth was that as a youngster Highpockets had always been an American Leaguer. He rooted hard for Washington and had a deep ambition to play for the Senators. The fact that the shoe might be on the other foot and the front office might not choose to keep him was a new idea. An upsetting one, too.

Naturally Spike did not know this. There was another thing the manager didn't know. Bryson

City fans had been planning to come north to celebrate Cecil McDade Day, and the whole state was chipping in to buy him a new automobile. A Cecil McDade Day with Cecil McDade not present would be awkward.

"The minors!" He was upset now. Every ballplayer who comes up knows that some day he must go down, but Highpockets was jolted. His dreams of the big salary, the seventy-thousand-dollar pay check, and the manager to handle his contracts and outside appearances like other stars, suddenly vanished.

"Certainly, the minors," said Spike quickly, pressing home the point. "What d'you expect? Think I'm going to hand you over to the Cubs or the Cards or the Braves to belt our brains out?"

Highpockets' composure returned. There was always Washington and the Senators. "Yeah . . . sure . . . I know . . . only . . . I mean, there's the American League."

Spike cut him short. "The boys wouldn't waiver you. Too many clubs in this-here league would like to get their mitts on you." He rose and lit a cigarette, went across to the window, came back and sat down facing his visitor.

"Anyhow, I'm not giving up on you yet. Fact is, I b'lieve you have a great future. I'm sure you'll learn and I want you with this club. But here's what you must do—you must learn to scatter those hits. How? I'm telling you. Every time you go up to the cage in batting drill you take four cuts. Right? Right! O.K. Bunt the first one to third and see you make it good. Hit the second to left, not hard, mind you; just punch it in there. Then if you want to, if you feel you'd like to, pull the next two to your natural hitting spot in right. Get it?"

The boy nodded. Spike continued. "You've got to conquer that weakness. You must learn to drag the ball once in a while, to hit to left field."

Highpockets' face was serious; he seemed to be thinking it over. Finally he murmured: "Bunt the first one to third. Hit the second to left field . . ."

"That's correct. And look, big boy, another thing. You've simply got to change your batting stance to stop that steady diet of inside pitching they're feeding you. Get out of those cleat marks. You stand there all set to slug the ball and you're a pushover for a smart pitcher. Move round so he'll be worried, so he won't be sure what you're aiming to do. You have unlimited possibilities, Highpockets; you cover ground, you catch any ball that isn't over the fence, and you're a power hitter. This thing is right up to you."

The next afternoon Highpockets went out to the cage and did exactly as he had been told. Four cuts —a smooth bunt tapped down toward third, a line drive smacked deftly into the open spaces in left field, and a couple of long ones that whanged against the concrete in right. Each one was perfectly met and well timed; he made it look so easy. The manager, watching with one hand on the dugout roof, felt pleased.

Nothing dumb about that bird; he's catching on; can't say the boy isn't smart. No, nothing the matter with him, nothing a little talking to won't straighten out. Why, he's a cinch compared to Jocko Klein and Roy and Bones Hathaway and some of the problems I've had on this man's ballclub.

Unfortunately Highpockets got away to a bad start that afternoon against the first-place Cards. In the first inning, after two had flied out, a St. Louis batter singled sharply to right over first base. It was a clothesline drive, and Highpockets loped across toward the foul line, making a one-handed stop of a ball that would have been through most outfielders for extra bases. The runner was taking his turn around the bag as he cut the ball off.

Highpockets stumbled a few steps forward and steadied himself to throw in, while the Redleg danced beyond first, watching his movements closely. The second his arm went back and he had committed himself to a throw to first, the baserunner turned and scurried at full speed for second. Too late, Highpockets saw the trick and burned in

his throw, which was hurried and high, forcing
Lester to jump. The first baseman reached for it
with his mitt, came down, and whirled to throw
to second. The ball got there just as the Cardinal
runner slid in head first under the toss.

The air was steaming with invective and abuse.
Strong and clear from the stands came the shrieks
and cries. From left and from right the wolves were
upon him.

"Hey, there, Highpockets, you rockhead, you!"

"Highpockets, you big bum!"

He turned on them and made a gesture which
was not exactly polite. The bleachers, delighted,
howled in unison. When the following batter singled
to center, scoring the man from second, the jeering
and yelling increased in volume. Up and down the
line they shouted and called to him as the inning
finished with the Cards ahead one to nothing, and
he came hustling in to the dugout.

"Hey, there, beanpole, you bum, you."

Though he paid no outward attention to the noise,
Highpockets was furious, piqued by the jeers of the
crowd, angry at baseball and everything and everyone connected with it. His face was still flushed
when his turn came in the batting order and he
stepped to the plate. The bags were full, Lester on
third, Roy Tucker dancing beside second, Paul Roth

on first. The bases full, nobody out, a chance to get that run back and put the game on ice.

A hit to left, even the easiest of rollers into that open space between third and second, would mean the game. He had determined to cross up the Card defense, not slug the ball, to pass up the home-run clout and punch the ball to left to help the team. But he was annoyed and upset by his blunder, and as he reached the plate the taunts of the mob rose all over the field. Highpockets forgot his resolution, forgot his determination to hit to left, and dug in in the batter's box, waving his war-club.

Knowing he loved fireball pitching, the Cardinal hurler kept throwing sliders and slow curves, teasing him with balls that asked to be hit, that hung up there and then slid off his bat at the last second. One he got a piece of and fouled. The next was a low pitch. A knuckler came over the edge of the plate for strike two as the crowd shrieked. A high inside pitch, another foul, another ball inside. The full count.

On the bags the runners danced with outstretched arms. From back of first, Red Cassidy yelled through his cupped hands. The commotion over the park was tremendous. Except for the third baseman, the Cardinal infield was camped on the right side, waiting for his conventional drive. The pitcher stood motionless in the box. His glove hung from his wrist;

he rubbed up the ball, gazing intently at his catcher behind the plate. He nodded with confidence and stepped to the rubber.

Highpockets set himself for that pay-off pitch. Furious with rage, he was going to hit the next one as no baseball had ever been hit before.

The pitcher raised his arms and threw. The ball was a high slider, and Highpockets swung hard from his heels, missed, and twisted clean around in a whirl that sent him sprawling backward, one arm behind to keep himself from falling to the ground.

The field resounded as he picked himself up from the dirt, slung his bat away in disgust, and slouched back to the dugout—to the far end of the dugout where no one at the moment happened to be sitting, where he was alone.

Chapter 7

THERE were three men aboard, no one out, the top of the batting order at the plate, and still they were unable to punch home a run. After Highpockets whiffed, Jocko Klein drove a scorching liner straight at the first baseman, who beat Paul Roth in the race back to the bag for a double-play. So the Cardinal hurler got out of the pickle vat, and from that moment had the Dodgers on the hip all the way.

Jimmie Duveen, the Card pitcher, had superb control that afternoon. His fast ball was alive, his curve breaking sharply. One Brooklyn batter after another went down swinging. There wasn't an inning when at least one man didn't strike out. After the door was slammed shut in their faces in the first, not a Dodger hitter reached base in the next three innings. In fact, nobody got as far as second until the seventh. Highpockets lined to deep right in the fourth and was passed purposely in the seventh after Roy had singled. However, the rest of the batting order was unable to get the ball out of the in-field and they were left on bases.

Disaster reached out its long arm for Brooklyn in the eighth. With two away, the St. Louis catcher worked Razzle for a base on balls, his second of the day. The pitcher, after setting himself for the ortho-dox bunt and missing, astonished the crowd by tak-ing a hefty swing at the next delivery. He caught one of Raz's fast pitches squarely and lifted it to deep right center.

Roy Tucker and Highpockets both went after it, though it was nearest Roy, who faded fast and charged back under the ball. Suddenly Highpockets realized that Roy was dangerously close to the wall.

"Watch it, Roy! Watch it, kid," he shouted. "Watch it, watch it!"

Roy either missed his call in the noise from above or paid no attention in his pursuit of the ball. Back he went, heedlessly, and stuck his glove up at the last second just as his head smacked the concrete. His body folded up and tumbled to the grass.

Highpockets raced over, not sure in the confu-sion of the moment whether or not Roy had man-aged to hold the ball. The umpire at second was also uncertain, and ran out to determine whether the catch had been made. All the while the runners, convinced it was a safe hit, circled the bags. Then the noise died away. The fans in the stands rushed to the rail, jamming forward to discover what had happened, looking down silently at the figure lying on the grass. For a few breathless seconds no one knew whether Roy was dead or alive.

It was Highpockets who reached him first, followed by the puffing umpire. Roy lay crumpled on the turf, completely out, the ball wedged securely in his glove. The crowd, unaware whether he had held it or not, let out a sudden tremendous yell as a big zero went up in the run column on the scoreboard in deep right.

Highpockets kneeled down by Roy's unconscious body. There was a gash in the forehead from which blood streamed. It splashed alarmingly on the white trousers of Highpockets' monkey suit. Now they were surrounded by players of both teams, pitchers from the Cardinal bullpen, Paul Roth, Spike and Bob Russell with anxious faces, and the Doc, who raced out from the dugout. He reached them, bent down, listened to Roy's heart, and felt his pulse. Then he rose, beckoning toward the plate. Instantly two groundsmen with a stretcher appeared, and for the second time in his career the Kid from Tomkinsville was carried off Ebbets Field unconscious. It was a tough break, and the Dodgers were grave as they gathered round the stretcher being taken in to the clubhouse.

Only Raz as usual was irrepressible.

"Someone ought to tell Roy there's no future in that," he remarked sagely. "What's more," and he glanced quickly at Highpockets shuffling along beside him as they followed the stretcher, "what's more, concrete costs money these days."

Highpockets' emotions were mixed. He liked Roy Tucker, one of the men on the club who had been agreeable and kind, one of the few players who seemed not to have forgotten his own rookie days. He felt the blow to the club and knew how serious it was to lose their star fielder. He also realized that through his own failure to follow instructions at bat he had not improved his standing with the manager of the Dodgers. Everyone on the club knew that Spike Russell meant what he said and never fooled around. However, the accident changed everything. Now the team was short a fielder. Therefore he himself was badly needed. They simply had to keep him in Brooklyn.

He pulled himself together, these thoughts racing through his brain, separating themselves into different feelings as he calculated the effect of the accident upon his own fortunes. Then he came to.

Razzle was glaring at him. He had half heard the pitcher's words and hastily assented. Concrete costs money these days.

"It does, doesn't it? Shore 'nough," he agreed solemnly.

Reports that filtered through from the clubhouse were none too definite. Roy had come to; but whether there was a concussion or merely a blow which had knocked him out temporarily was impossible to tell until he reached the hospital and X-rays were taken. As they stepped in for the ninth, grabbing their bats from the rack, they could hear above the hum and buzz over the field the CLANG-CLANG of the ambulance charging full speed down Bedford Avenue out beyond the right field fence.

Lester Young, the first batter, grounded out. With only two more to get, the Cards snapped the ball smoothly and confidently around the infield. Old Swanny, taking Roy's spot, then came up with his menacing bat and promptly belted the first pitch to right for a single. Alan Whitehouse was sent in to run for him, and the early departers stood in the exits watching, as Paul Roth sacrificed and Alan took second base.

So they were down to their last out of the game when Highpockets rose from his knee in the circle. Even before he reached the plate, the hurricane of noise began. The crowd was in a savage mood. They wanted badly to win that game, and they were annoyed with Highpockets for his mistake in the first inning which had led to the only score. They were disappointed at the failure of the Brooks to hit; they were upset and worried at losing the favorite member of the club, the Kid from Tomkinsville. When, therefore, Highpockets stepped to the plate, they gave him a gigantic razoo from every side of the field.

"You murderer," shouted one fan who had failed to hear him warn Roy off the fence. "You murderer, Highpockets!" It was the worst riding of the season. Jeers, croaks, howls, and moans echoed over the ballpark. They bothered him not at all. For the first time that day, Highpockets was assured and poised. Obviously, with Roy injured, he was a fixture in right field. Now he was certain of a Cecil McDade Day and that new Ford cabriolet. After that, as to the seventy-thousand-dollar contract and the manager for his outside appearances, well, anything could happen and he wasn't exactly the worrying kind.

So he set himself in the box, loose and secure. As he stood there the jeers died away only to grow in volume when he looked at the first pitch, which was dead across the plate. The raspberry continued and became larger still as he took a ball and then fouled off the next one. It began to have an effect upon his nerves. Suddenly he determined to show them up, every one of them, the whole ballpark. The derision of the mob acted as a stimulant. No longer was he lunging and hitting wildly. He was angry now, tense with a flaming desire to smash that ball down his hecklers' throats.

It was a pitch with just a little bit of extra fat on it, fast and outside, and he swung hard. The ball was wide of the plate, so accidentally he hit, not to right as usual, but to left. Not a line drive to the outfield or a grasscutter into the open spaces between second and third, but a terrific clout that was really tagged. The stands gasped. Every player on the field knew by the sound it was in there. Alan, galloping around third base, turned his head to watch the ball drop into Section 30, in the upper tier of the stands in deep left center.

Highpockets loped around the bases. Now the jeers of the crowd changed to frantic cheers. He actually had driven that ball down their open throats. They yelled and shouted and threw newspapers and scorecards and things into the air. The noise was sweet music to him as he rounded third base and touched home plate, reaching out for Jocko Klein's extended hand as he stomped across the platter. Without in the least slackening his pace, he tore for the dugout and the passageway under the stands that led to the clubhouse and the showers.

Jocko was the only man on the club who waited for him to complete the circuit. By the time Highpockets reached the dugout it was empty.

Chapter 8

THERE were only three ways to play him, and different managers adopted different tactics. You could walk him. Lots of hurlers did whenever men were on base. Or you could pitch to him and hope for the best. But the majority of pilots packed the defense on the right side. As they reasoned, it was far better to let him try for the single or the occasional grounder to left, and if he made it you were no worse off than if you passed him. Moreover, there was better than an even chance that he would fly out or drive a liner at an infielder in right.

By the middle of July, Highpockets was batting .305 and had made twenty-seven homers. The team, however, was still anchored in fifth place, and folks in Brooklyn stopped asking every night how the Brooks made out. They simply inquired, "What did Highpockets do today?"

With an open date the club was traveling home from Cincinnati to play a postponed game against the New York Giants, and at the same time to celebrate Cecil McDade Day. That evening on the train Highpockets found himself unable to sleep, and about eleven o'clock wandered out to the club car for a sandwich and a glass of milk. Jocko Klein was reading a magazine as he dropped into the adjoining seat.

"Why, now, that's a good idea. Think I could use the same," said Jocko, when he heard his teammate give the order to the waiter. They were munching away a few minutes later when Charlie Draper came into the car with George McPherson, the club secretary. He passed the two men chatting over their sandwiches, and stood hesitating a minute before them.

"O.K., you boys. O.K. Only understand, you're here strictly on your own." The ballplayers glanced at him and the secretary continued. "I mean the club isn't picking up the check on this; it buys your meals, not your late lunches."

They said nothing and he moved along to the far end of the car with Draper. In a few minutes the waiter brought the check, and Jocko started to dig for his wallet.

"Hold it, Jocko," said Highpockets, laying a restraining hand on the other's arm. Then he reached across for the check, picked it up, and rose. Jocko looked after him with a puzzled gaze. What's that crazy busher up to now!

Slowly Highpockets walked down the swaying car to the table where the road secretary sat playing fan-tan with the coach, a bottle of beer between them.

"Hey there, George." The secretary raised his eyes. "Twenty-seven homers. Get it?" He laid the check, face down, on the table. The secretary was not slow on the uptake. He picked up the check, while Highpockets went back along the swinging car to his room in the rear of the train.

The next afternoon was an event in Brooklyn. Cecil McDade Day drew a delegation from Bryson City and a larger one from North Carolina; it also attracted a capacity crowd of customers from the environs of Greater New York, who arrived armed with tin whistles, cowbells, horns, and other instruments of noise-making to join in the fun. They yelled and yammered at Highpockets, and their cries were warmer and more friendly than usual. Which did not mean that as paying clients they relinquished the right to shout abuse whenever the occasion arose.

The Brooks were spread out in practice over the park before the game, and Highpockets was hounding the deep fungos from Charlie Draper's stick, when he was approached by a man with a camera over his shoulder.

"Mr. McDade?" he said, briskly.

"Yessuh." Highpockets stopped, breathing heavily from his last race for the ball.

"Davis from *Life Magazine.* We're planning to run a double-page spread on you late this summer, and I'd appreciate a chance to get some shots."

Highpockets glanced at him with curiosity, and noticed that he was better dressed than the newspaper photographers who swarmed around the baselines and infested the clubhouse after important games. Moreover he lacked the cigar or the end thereof which most newspaper cameramen usually wore in their mouths.

"Where d'you say you came from?" He merely wanted to be sure. A fellow could make mistakes easy in things of this sort.

"*Life Magazine,*" replied the man, unslinging his camera in a businesslike way. "Like to get some action pictures of you out here in the field, some close-ups, and a few good shots of you at the bat. Oh, yes, and some time this next week can we make an appointment to take you informally in your hotel room?"

"Yessuh. I'll shore be glad to accommodate you." He spoke courteously, but all the while he was thinking. *Life Magazine.* H'm, those boys have the dough. "Yessuh," he said. "For two hundred and fifty dollars."

The camera, half unslung, almost slipped from

the photographer's grasp. He hesitated, glanced up at the gangling youth in the monkey suit to see whether he meant it, replaced the machine on his shoulder, and then without a word turned and walked away.

The fans in right had been watching the affair with attention. Not knowing precisely who the man was or what had happened, they gave the photographer the raspberry as he came slowly in toward the plate, past the stands.

Meanwhile Highpockets went back to chasing fungos against the fences. Yes, sir, a fellow sure does need a manager up here in the big time.

Most ballplayers dislike presentation ceremonies and special days, although none to date has ever been known to refuse a leather traveling case, much less a Ford cabriolet. However, the occasion as a rule affects their play. They become embarrassed, tighten up, fumble at the plate and stumble in the field. Not Highpockets. To him Cecil McDade Day was merely another afternoon of baseball with good friends from home along to see the fun. Except, that is, for the shiny, red Ford cabriolet. The car, well sheathed in ribbons and streamers, with the state flag attached to the bonnet and the top down, was driven slowly around the ballpark by the daughter of the Governor, an attractive blonde. Then the ceremonies of the day began.

The boys on the two clubs stood on the dugout steps, while the shouts and yells of the crowd rose in volume. That day, however, the approbation exceeded the cynical taunts from the stands. For, after all, few fans could completely laugh off a man who had bashed out twenty-seven homers in the first three months of the season.

In tones that were warm and homelike to Highpockets after months of nasal northern accents, the Governor presented him with the keys to the car. The Tar Heels clustered around the plate. They were glad to see him and he was gratefully pleased to see them. Some he had known (and some only by name) in Bryson City; Mr. Smith, the druggist; Mr. Barnewell, the president of the bank; and Mr. Harrison, the lawyer who had offices in Tuttle's Block. Several of them spoke, and everyone said the same thing in different words. They were proud to have a Bryson City boy make good in the majors, and they had come north to tell him so.

Then the announcer, in the identical tones he used to talk about a new mouthwash or introduce a refrigerator, called on Highpockets in a tremendous din. It finally died away. He leaned far down over the nickel amplifier. His self-possession did not desert him, and if his speech of acceptance was not a lengthy affair, it had the merit of saying what he meant, and his voice was clear and direct over the entire park.

"Folks . . . and friends . . . I thank you all very kindly. I'm shore obliged to you all for coming up here this afternoon and for giving me this beautiful car. I appreciate it, I shore do."

He turned and shook hands with the Governor and several of the men around home plate. The radio announcer switched the program back to the control room, for the affair had been broadcast over the network, and that was that. The ceremonies for the day were finished; the ball game, the important thing and especially important when Dodgers meet Giants, could start.

All the while, kneeling on the ground around the batter's box, their cameras pointed at Highpockets like a battery of machine guns, were the photographers. They wore grimy polo shirts open at the neck, and the majority had desiccated cigar butts in their mouths. The elegant man from *Life Magazine* was not among the kneeling throng.

Chapter 9

THE things Highpockets recalled afterward about Cecil McDade Day were two, neither one connected with the presentation ceremonies nor the things that were said about him there. The first pertained to the contest. It wasn't the lucky two-bagger off the handle of his bat, but the fly ball which cost the Brooks the game.

It happened in the sixth inning of a scoreless tie and let in the only run of the game. The day was bright and hazy in turn. At times the sun burned through an overcast, at times it would slide under the clouds. Ten minutes later it would come out in full force.

The whole game dragged along. Every inning seemed to last an hour, for Jerry Fielding in the box for the Dodgers was always a slow pitcher, and that day took plenty of time on every batter. Receiving the ball, he would toss his glove off and stand rubbing up the sphere with both palms for several seconds. Next he would lean carefully over for the rosin bag, dust off his meat hand, toss the bag behind and, stepping to the rubber, stand motionless until he got the sign from Jocko behind the plate. A nod, a peck at the brim of his cap, a look around the bags, a measured sweep of his hand across the shirt. At last he was set to throw.

At the start of the sixth, the day was gloomy. Highpockets, who had been fiddling with his sun glasses on the bench, discovered that he had dropped them and left them there. Instead of stopping the game and asking for them, he said nothing. After the first two batters were out on infield grounders, the sun suddenly broke through, strong and clear. Jerry tired, his control failed for a moment, he threw four balls and passed the third hitter. The next man hit to right field, an easy out that Highpockets sighted and then lost completely in the brilliant sunshine. From the stands, indeed from the playing field, it simply seemed that he was lazy. For he ambled slowly backward, loping along while the ball dropped a few feet beyond his reach on what should have been a sure put-out. And the last of the inning.

With two down, the runner on first was naturally off as the ball was struck. He galloped past Spike Russell at short, who was watching his right fielder loaf after the fly and miss the catch by a yard. The manager stood roundly cursing Highpockets for a conceited busher and a clumsy clown.

Hang it, he thought, hang it all. If this was only an ordinary game today, I'd yank him for that so quick he'd never know what struck him. I sure would.

The bewildered boy in right finally sighted the ball as it got past and out of the sun. Before he could reach it, however, the runner had scored, and the batter was safely perched on second base. An important tally went up on the scoreboard, while the crowd turned to watch whether a hit or an error would be given on the play. The lenient score-keeper signaled a hit, but no one on the club was fooled by that, nor in the stands either.

Not realizing that he had lost the ball in the sun without his glasses, the stands rose, jeering. From all sides came the abuse.

"Hey, there, dogface!"

"Yoo-hoo, Cecil, yoo-hoo!"

"Highpockets, you bum, you; you bum, High-pockets!"

They kept after him whenever he was in the field or at bat during the remainder of the game, which ended one to nothing for New York.

Spike Russell was furious. He made a point of never calling players down directly after a game when he himself was usually in a tense frame of mind. But that afternoon he issued a most unusual order. He closed the clubhouse to everyone, even the newspapermen attached to the team.

The boys showered and dressed in grim silence. Highpockets, more miserable than anyone, hardly knew what to say or how to explain his misfortune. I pulled a rock, he thought, as he sat in his dripping clothes. I sure pulled a rock today. Nobody guessed how disaster had overtaken him or even queried him about it. So he sat glumly on the bench before his locker as the others trooped past to the showers.

Bones Hathaway was the only one who spoke to him. Bones had spent the afternoon on the bench, watching. He came from the showers as Highpockets, naked save for a towel around his shanks, at last moved toward them. The pitcher stopped and faced him squarely.

"Hey, look, Highpockets. Just one thing. You'll never do that to me."

The big chap hesitated. His face flushed, his temper flared. He was not afraid of a fight. He wanted to slug it out with Bonesey because of the implied accusation. Then he changed his mind, tried to explain, to say something, to admit his mistake; then he changed his mind again. Face-to-face they stood there, the tall, powerful pitcher and the lanky rookie with the taller frame and the hefty pair of shoulders. Enemies now. And both members of the same club.

Highpockets' fists tightened on the towel about his waist. He moved past into the showers without a word.

The second thing he never forgot about Cecil McDade Day cost more than a game of baseball. He was to be entertained that evening at dinner in a Manhattan hotel by the Tar Heel delegation, and he was leaving the clubhouse alone when the head groundsman entered and asked what he wanted done with his car.

The car? The car? Of course, the car! Have to take it somewhere. He hated the car already; he wished they had never given him the car. But there the car was. The only thing he could think of was to drive to his hotel and have the doorman send it round to his hotel garage. He discovered it parked near the exit in center field that led to Bedford Avenue. The Ford was devoid of flags and banners, yet still red, shiny, elegant in the afternoon sun.

Several attendants were watching as he stepped in, fishing out his keys, and started the motor. He knew perfectly what they were thinking, so he hastily threw the clutch in and moved forward, pausing as they opened the gate. The car stalled. It took some few minutes to get it going once more because the carburetor was flooded. Several kids passing by saw and recognized him immediately. They leaped to the running board, begging for his autograph. The groundsman shooed them away. Highpockets finally started the motor and jerked out into the traffic pouring down Bedford Avenue.

He was exhausted physically and emotionally from the long afternoon. It was also the first time he had ever driven in the traffic of a large city. So he went cautiously along in the rush and roar of the late afternoon crush, stalling frequently at traffic lights, collecting curses from taxi drivers and queer looks from people in passing cars who knew exactly where they were headed. Finally he turned off and found himself in a comparatively quiet section of residential dwellings. Cars were parked along each side of the street, but he stopped, got out, and asked a policeman for directions.

Hardly had the cop, in language he found difficult to understand, finished, when there was an annoyed squawk from the rear. The red cabriolet with the top down was blocking a large truck that happened to be parked by the curb just behind him. Highpockets thanked the officer hastily, jumped into his car, and quickly started the motor. It immediately stalled. There was a series of angry honks, and, glancing back in the mirror, he saw an evil-browed man with a cap on one side of his head and a cigar in his mouth, behind the wheel of the truck.

For a second or so the ballplayer was so exasperated he had an immense desire to step out and slug the ugly driver. He refrained. The car moved off with that inevitable jerk, going down the street at a lively clip, pursued by the truck, from whose exhaust issued roars and explosions.

Several hundred feet beyond, an ancient car was parked by the curb at the right. A man slid from the front seat just before the red cabriolet drew abreast, got out and, opening the hood, peered within. Seconds later, exactly as the two cars were side by side, a boy raced out from the sidewalk.

Highpockets felt a horrible bump as the boy smashed into the Ford's right fender and heard a sickening sound of something falling. The youngster disappeared from sight.

It happened so quickly. First he was riding along, no one was there, nothing in front of the car. Then the boy dived out from the side, hit the car, and all at once he was gone, he had vanished. He was nowhere.

There was the fierce squealing of the brakes. His car stopped so suddenly that Highpockets was thrown against the wheel. He leaped out and rushed back, his knees trembling, sweat on his forehead. A boy, red of face, was stretched unconscious on the pavement beside the ancient car. The man leaned over the boy. He looked up.

"Here, mister, help me. You take his legs. Nope, wait a minute, mebbe we better leave him here . . . No, let's carry him to the curb. You're all right, Dean, you're O.K., boy."

Quite plainly the man was as upset as Highpockets. He had no idea what to do next. He, too, was frightened by the suddenness of the accident. The ballplayer bent down. The face of the youngster was smeared with grease, one leg was bleeding badly, his trousers were torn, there was blood across his right arm. He was silent, terrifyingly silent.

Is he badly hurt? Or stunned? Or seriously injured? Or killed? Highpockets stood there, unable to act, unable to move.

Then all at once the kid began to cry. Hurt he was, badly injured he might well be. But certainly he was not dead. His crying had a strong and healthy sound. A welcome one, also, for a feeling of enormous relief rose within the ballplayer.

"Look! He can't lie here like this. We better take him to the curb and get a doc right off." He leaned over and lifted the boy's legs while the father picked up his shoulders. The youngster bawled louder and louder still as they lugged him clumsily to the sidewalk and laid him down.

Highpockets stood wiping his face, looking at the tousled lad, thinking that while he might not be dead he was probably badly injured. Highpockets was miserable. He knew that he had been going too fast for that crowded street, that if he had not been upset he would have been driving at a slower pace and the blow would have been less severe.

In a minute half a dozen kids had collected, and behind the circle surrounding the sobbing boy on the pavement, Highpockets recognized the truck driver with the cigar still in his mouth. Then a policeman sauntered up.

"Lemme see yer license, bud," he said, casually. He was quite unconcerned about the accident. Apparently this sort of thing happened frequently in Brooklyn.

The father spoke up for the first time. "It's nothing, nothing much, officer. He's not hurt bad. This gentleman ain't to blame." At this remark the youngster howled louder than ever. The circle around them grew rapidly. Boys' voices spoke up. "It's Dean. Dean Kennedy. He's had an accident." Windows opened, heads appeared above and across the street.

Highpockets had only a North Carolina license, which fortunately was in his wallet. He handed it over; the policeman glanced at it and handed it back. He grunted.

"That-there your car?"

Highpockets nodded.

"O.K. I'll call an ambulance," said the officer.

"Ambulance! We live near here. Look, he's not that bad, officer," said the boy's father.

"Yeah, we better be sure. I'll just call the Bushwick; they ain't too far from here. Leave him lie there. You never know is they any broken bones. Leave him lie . . ." He turned and walked a hundred feet to the red police box on the corner. They saw him open it up with a key and with no apparent hurry, and take the telephone off the hook.

Then the truck driver edged his way through the circle, animosity on his face. "Hey, youse, you Cecil McDade of the Dodgers?"

You run over a kid with your car; you make him lose a leg possibly; you hurt him surely; you lay him up certainly for a long, long time. Just a kid, lying there crying on the pavement. So you forget things, sort of; your job is a long way off. So, too, are your home and your people.

Then you're brought suddenly back to Brooklyn. Highpockets, disconsolate and worried, turned to nod. He disliked Brooklyn more than ever he had before. He wished with all his heart he had never seen Flatbush. Or the Dodgers, either.

"Ya bum!" said the truck driver, venom in his tones. "Whatcha wanna drop that fly against the G'ints for this afternoon?"

Cecil McDade of the Dodgers! There was a kind

of involuntary forward movement all around the circle as the boys on the edge pressed toward him, curiosity on every face. The injured youngster ceased to bawl. The father, kneeling beside him, looked up quickly. Cecil McDade! Why, say, that's Highpockets.

It was the truck driver who spoke. "Ya bum ya! If that hadda been you out there just now, know what I'd'a done? I'd'a run over ya. Yeah, an' they'd gimme a pension fer life instead of sending me to jail, too."

Chapter 10

SPORTSWRITERS on metropolitan dailies from one end of the league to the other had interviewed Highpockets and obtained little more information than could be found in the pages of the *Baseball Guide*. Radio commentators, despite their sticky persistence, had no better success. The visit of the Tar Heel delegation to Manhattan was therefore an opportunity the New York reporters seized eagerly. Many sporting columns appeared the morning after Cecil McDade Day in Brooklyn, all concerned with Highpockets and all written before the accident. These stories were mostly accounts of his life in the environs of Bryson City and his early baseball career. A few newspapers even ran photographs of the McDade family on the farm at home. Like the rest of his craft, Casey had talked with the businessmen from North Carolina. Moreover, his observant eyes had seen the photographer rebuffed on the field before the game. Some little investigation plus a few telephone calls gave Casey an opening lead for his column the next day.

The tale is running around that the human umbrella who plays right field for the Brooks knows how to handle himself in a broken field. The other day when told that he had been chosen, with Manager Spike Russell and Catcher Jocko Klein, to play in the All-Star game in Cincinnati next week, he accepted the unusual honor with this crack: "Yeah. All-Star games don't put no groceries on the table." And when *Life Magazine* sent a photographer around to get a series of pictures of him recently, Highpockets is said to have demanded the sum of two hundred and fifty dollars for the privilege of snapping his phiz. At first sight it may seem amazing for *Life,* an institution used to having its own way, to be held up by a farm boy from North Carolina. Thinking it over, however, one has to admit that nobody helped Cecil McDade on his journey up from the minors, and it is not likely that *Life Magazine* would offer him a job as executive editor if his eyes go and he loses that home-run punch.

Everyone knows the toothpick squeezes a nickel harder than most ballplayers hold on to a twenty-five cent tip; but investigation among the North Carolinians in the city for Cecil McDade Day yesterday proves there's a reason. You'll never get this from Highpockets himself; however, it appears he lives on a hilly farm in the red clay soil of Rabbit Creek up back of town, on land which until lately grew only sour corn and not a lot of that. He is saving to buy fertilizer and livestock to make the place a producing farm, and also to give an education that he never received to his five brothers and sisters. There is no sense pretending that the bean-pole is the most popular man on the Brooklyn club, either with the fans or his teammates; yet if some of the latter knew more about his background, they might be understanding in a way they are not at the present time.

Highpockets read all this on the subway going over to the hospital the next morning with no pleas-urable emotion. Shoot, those birds, those sports-writers! Always after an angle. Why don't they let a guy alone! He tossed the paper down, grateful for only one thing about the events of the past day. Directly after the accident, he had called George McPherson, the club secretary, and fortunately reached him at home. An old newspaperman him-self, George went into action immediately. He spent several feverish hours at police headquarters, at the hospital, and on the telephone. After considerable effort had been expended and various wires pulled, all traces of the event were submerged from even the inquisitive eyes of Casey himself. No one but the few directly concerned would know about the affair unless one of the participants talked out of turn. Highpockets had no fear of breaking down himself.

So he went to the hospital thinking of this with relief, thankful also that it was a boy who had been injured rather than a girl. Boys understand baseball; we'll have something in common, he felt. Actually, Highpockets' knowledge of metropolitan youth was confined mostly to the kids who pestered him for autographs, who lined up along the wire netting outside the runway from the dugout to the clubhouse at Ebbets Field, kids who knew the batting averages and records of every player on the club. They, and their counterparts in other cities of the league, were the kind of youngsters he pictured as American boys. To his amazement, Dean Kennedy was another type. Certainly if he was agitated at entertaining a man who had hit thirty homers, he failed to show it.

In fact, conversation between the ballplayer and the boy was not exactly spontaneous. The athlete sat on a stiff chair beside the bed. The kid lay motionless, his blue eyes fixed solemnly on his visitor, a sort of tent of bedclothes over his injured leg, which, so the nurses said, was healing nicely. They had already suggested to Highpockets that the patient might be home in a few days. After ascertaining that the youngster felt all right and had no pain or internal injuries, Highpockets launched into the only subject except farming that he himself knew well. That was his profession.

The American as against the National League, ever a favorite subject of discussion for sport fans, drew no comment whatever from the lad. The pennant race in the National, a red hot affair in which seven and a half games separated the tail-enders and leaders, failed to produce a spark. Even the chances of the Dodgers left the boy unmoved. Highpockets was working hard now, talking far more than ever he talked to the most pertinacious newshound. There was little response. The boy replied with a yes or no.

"Look," Highpockets asked in despair, "who's yer favorite team in the National?"

"I d'know."

"Well, I mean, haven't you got a favorite team? Mebbe you're an American Leaguer?"

"Nope," said the boy. He apparently wasn't interested in either league.

"See here," said the ballplayer, somewhat exasperated, "d' you mean to tell me you aren't a ball fan?"

The boy in the bed shook his mane of yellow hair. He seemed to feel no special regret for his ignorance, or shame because he lived in Brooklyn and had no affection for the Dodgers. Highpockets was rocked. He had heard of such youngsters, and he presumed there must be some kids who didn't really care for big league baseball; but he had never met them. He was astonished and a little upset, too. Pursued by boys and girls through every hotel lobby in every town in the circuit, assaulted as he left every ballpark by a bevy of kids with pencils in their outstretched hands, he assumed all right-thinking American boys read the *Sporting News* and collected small cards several inches square with photographs of ballplayers and their names underneath.

CECIL "HIGHPOCKETS" McDADE
Right Field, Brooklyn, N.L.

To find one who didn't, and in Brooklyn, of all places! For a minute he hardly knew how to proceed.

"You mean to tell me you aren't interested in baseball? That's strange. How come?"

"I d'know," said the boy calmly. He wasn't interested. That was that and he felt no shame about it.

The silence in the room lengthened. As a rule Highpockets enjoyed these pauses in conversation immensely. He liked them especially when he found himself cornered on the bench before the game, because these silences meant his tormentor was running out of stupid questions and getting near the end of the interview. This silence was different. Now he was on the receiving end, instead of the other way round.

A boy who doesn't like baseball! Imagine that! Highpockets observed that the books and games he had carefully selected to be sent to the lad were piled up on a side table, apparently unopened and untouched. Even the life story of the new strike-out hero of the American League had failed to interest this unusual youngster.

Highpockets dropped baseball with regret. In despair he asked, "What school d'you go to, Dean?"

"Franklin."

"What grade you in?"

"Eighth."

Well, that's something. For the first time since entering the room the ballplayer felt on surer ground. "That so, that so? Now, I have a kid brother down home in Bryson City, boy 'bout your age; he's in the eighth, too. Then most likely you'll go to high school next fall."

"Yeah."

The patient seemed less than enthusiastic about his promotion, yet Highpockets had no choice save to proceed along the same conversational road. "Well, now, what d'ya study in school, Dean?"

He ran his fingers nervously through his tousled hair. "Oh, I d'know. English. History. Oh, an' geogerfy, too."

"Which d'you like best?" At this point Highpockets began to feel like a reporter assaulting a baseball star with a series of senseless questions, talking merely to keep things going, hoping to strike on an angle for a story. An angle, an angle, that's what they were all after as they asked those stupid questions, invariably the same ones. How did it feel . . . your greatest thrill . . . what do you find different in the majors . . .

Suddenly he realized that he too was asking the lad in the bed the same sort of questions. For the first time Highpockets understood why sometimes sportswriters left him after an interview with a worried look upon their faces; for the first time he had some slight feeling of sympathy for those pests of the baseball world. It was a revolutionary idea, although Highpockets hardly appreciated this at the moment.

"Oh . . . I guess . . . geogerfy. We study that book . . . now . . . *Our World Today.*"

This was the first time the boy had volunteered a thing. Naturally the ballplayer had never heard of the book, so that topic was soon finished.

"Well, what d'you study next year in high school?"

Again that apathetic glance and the everlasting, "I d'know."

Highpockets was really discouraged. This was work, real hard work. He thought of his own kid brother, same age, same blue eyes, same yellow hair sticking up straight that never seemed to have been combed. Only if Henry Lee were in the same room with, say, Roy Tucker or Harry Chase of the Giants or Razzle Nugent, he would be sitting up straight, talking. He could talk with them, too, for he knew the batting averages of everyone in the league last year, and when they came up, and how. What he didn't know, which would be little, it wouldn't have taken him long to discover. Henry Lee McDade was a question machine from which questions poured endlessly whenever baseball was at issue. The questions usually came so fast he could hardly ask them, one after another, in such excitement that he stumbled and stuttered slightly as he tried in his haste to find out everything he wanted to know: what really happened in the third game of the '44 Series, and whether Raz minded pitching to left-handed batters, and what kind of a manager Spike Russell was, an' was he a better manager than Spunky Stowell of the Braves, an' . . . an' . . . an' . . .

He heard his brother's high-pitched tones, saw his tense face, his concentrated, wide-open eyes. This boy was different. What did he like, what interested him, how on earth could you talk with such a kid? The ballplayer became aware of the faintest tinge of respect for his enemies, the sports-writers, a feeling that was distinctly novel. It must be like this interviewing that rookie Ted Harkins of the White Sox and Judson Strong of the Cards. Yep, and Highpockets McDade of the Brooks, too.

He also discovered that he had assumed a knowledge of kids he did not possess. The whole thing was disconcerting. The silence persisted. The kid ran his fingers through his mop of hair and said nothing, which didn't help.

Highpockets rose. "Gotta be going. Gotta get moving. I'm playing in the All-Star game in Cincinnati tomorrow night."

He paused just to let this fact sink in. Still Dean was unimpressed. 823,365 votes, playing in the All-Star his first season in the majors, yet to this solemn-faced boy he was just another tiresome adult asking the same stuffy questions. What school d'you go to? What grade you in? What d'you study? Something was wrong. For most kids in Brooklyn this would be a big moment, perhaps the biggest moment of their lives, an event they'd talk about in school for years. Yet the youngster in the bed was bored. Perhaps unconsciously Highpockets had pictured himself as the home run king, visiting kids in the hospital and leaving them cheered and encouraged merely by his presence. Only things somehow weren't working out that way.

Highpockets felt uncomfortable. He was glad when a nurse entered with a glass of orange juice. The boy took it without a word, and glanced at the ballplayer across the edge of the glass with wide, curious eyes.

"Well, s'long. Anything you want . . . anything

you'd like . . . you need?" His gaze wandered again toward the table and his unopened books stacked there.

The boy shook his head and said nothing.

"O.K. I'll be back here the first of the week. Get yerself well and outa this-here hospital before I come back, y'understand?"

"Yeah."

"Well, g'by now."

"G'by."

The boy still looked at him over the rim of the glass as he left. Highpockets walked down the corridor mopping his forehead.

Say! Maybe those sportswriters don't have such a soft touch after all.

Chapter 11

WHEN you're free and loose and nothing depends on it, that's when you can really play baseball. At the start of the afternoon, the parishioners in the right field bleachers at Crosley Field jeered and poured abuse, as the crowds did everywhere all over the circuit whenever Highpockets first took his place at bat or in the outer garden. He reacted to their noise by belting one into the stands against Seaman McNutt of the Yanks his first time at bat. He was passed in the fourth, and when he came up in the seventh the tone of the crowd had changed. This time he hit a terrific clout into the stands in right, known as "Giles' Picnic Grounds." Cincinnati sportswriters said a blow like that hadn't been hit there since the days of Babe Ruth.

Highpockets' first thought was to call the hospital as soon as he reached New York. From the start there was something strange about that telephone call: the long silences, the way everyone from the main operator to the head nurse kept asking his name and who he was and putting him off and passing him along to someone else. Except for the fact that the youngster was still hospitalized, he couldn't get a lot of information. Suddenly a supervisor of some sort came on the wire.

"Hold on a minute, please. Dr. Jansen is in the hospital now. I'll let you talk with him." Click-click, went the operator, click-click.

This is awful. Maybe something has happened to the boy. Must be the kid is worse. If only I hadn't lost my temper with the truck driver and started down the street so fast; if only I hadn't muffed that fly ball that day. If . . . if . . . if . . .

A voice asked whether Dr. Jansen was there, whether Dr. Jansen had come down from Surgery, and finally in tired tones someone answered, "Dr. Jansen."

"Oh, Doctor, this Cecil McDade."

"Who?"

"Cecil McDade, yessuh. I'm inquiring about Dean Kennedy, the boy who was injured last week in an auto accident. Hurt his leg, remember?"

"Oh, yes, oh, yes, I remember. You're the man who . . . yes, I remember now." There was an unpleasant pause. "Ah, that didn't turn out quite so well, not quite as we all expected."

Highpockets hardly knew what to say. He was

stunned. If only I'd kept my temper with that taxi driver, and had started off more slowly. "Yessuh. Is he still there in the hospital?"

"Yes, he is. You see that case didn't turn out the way we hoped. The boy has osteomyelitis."

"Has what? What's that?"

"Osteomyelitis. An inflammation of the bone in his leg has set in that necessitates an operation. We'll probably operate tomorrow. Though we haven't told him yet."

"Tomorrow? Is it serious?"

"Well, of course it could be. Fortunately we've got him in time, and I anticipate no complications. He's a healthy boy. Naturally, any operation . . . one never knows . . . you understand."

Highpockets was dizzy when he hung up. There was sweat over his forehead. Nothing I could have done would have prevented his smashing into my car; it wasn't my fault, it was his fault. Look, it really wasn't my fault. I was only going twenty . . . well, maybe thirty . . . I think . . . I honestly believe it wasn't over thirty. Osteomyelitis. Sounds bad. If only I hadn't dropped that fly or got mad with the truck driver; if only they'd never given me the darn car. I wish I'd never seen the Ford. But it wasn't my fault. You have to be reasonable in these things; it wasn't my fault and everyone said so;

his own dad said so; the boy ran straight off the curb into the car. Like that.

Highpockets went out into the street. He did something he seldom did, especially when subways were running. He hailed a taxi.

"Bushwick Hospital in Brooklyn." All the way over he was thinking. If only I'd held on to that fly and not been upset, if I'd kept my temper when that goon honked at me from his truck, if only . . .

The boy was wider-eyed than ever, somewhat paler and quite as unresponsive as the previous week. Meanwhile the fame of his visitor plus the two homers in the All-Star at Cincinnati still meant nothing to him. In several minutes, however, his father came along. Highpockets was relieved to have the man greet him with a delight that also had respect in it. He, at any rate, had heard of the Dodgers. Notwithstanding the impending operation, of which he knew, he again absolved the ballplayer of blame for the accident.

The victim glanced from one to the other with a wide-eyed stare, saying nothing and not missing a word. Then the nurse entered with a pill for her patient. Highpockets immediately noticed a change in her attitude. The previous week the boy had been an occupied bed, a nuisance, a kid who could easily be taken care of at home. Now he was a potential surgical case and possibly something more. For one never knew about operations.

The father was talking. He asked the boy whether he had thanked Mr. McDade for the lovely flowers, the baseball books, and the games which were heaped up, unopened still, on the side table. No? Had he written to thank him then? No, the boy had not. Mr. McDade was thanked somewhat sullenly in mumbled tones. Next the father thanked him, and then there was another one of those pauses.

At last came the usual, the inevitable, query: What's the matter with the Dodgers? Highpockets pointed out that although they were in fourth place, they were only six games off on the losing side, not bad for the end of July. Sometimes, he explained, it was harder to lead the league, to set the pace, than to come from behind. The father was interested and attentive, if the boy was not. He declared with enthusiasm that he was a great Dodger fan, and had seen Highpockets hit his sixteenth homer against the Cards and his twenty-first against the Phils.

"Never dreamed I'd ever get to meet you, though," he said, as if it was an honor to have his son run over by Highpockets. The ballplayer accepted this. Then conversation died away again. Highpockets became desperate. He tried to say something.

"Kinda funny, Mr. Kennedy, you living in Brooklyn and being interested in baseball, but this boy doesn't seem to care one bit."

The father turned on him. "All the time, all the time, Mr. Hi . . . Mr. McDade, that boy spends on his stamps. Won't work at school nor play ball nor anything. I've tried to send him to camp this summer; he won't go. And I've told him if he doesn't get to work and pass next year in high school, I'll take his stamps away. I sure will."

The boy sat up. The change in his expression was amazing. For the first time the youngster seemed alive. Then his face twisted; he was almost in tears. "Aw, Dad, you can't do that. Besides, I do so work in school, I do so. I got an A in geogerfy."

"Geography! Geography! Yes, and how 'bout your 'rithmetic and English and history? Geography! That's all you think of, that and your stamps. What I'm gonna do with him, I'm sure I don't know."

The boy ignored the remark and addressed a question to the ballplayer. It was the first time he had spoken to him directly. "You c'llect stamps?" There was a note of hopefulness in his voice.

"Collect stamps? Why, no, I never did. To tell you the fact, I never did collect stamps." Strange boy, thought Highpockets. Lives in Brooklyn, collects stamps, and isn't interested in the Dodgers!

The boy paid no attention. "I'll show you my c'llection."

The father interrupted. "No, Dean, no. He isn't interested in stamps."

"Sure, sure, I'd like for to see his collection very much indeed. Where is it?"

The collection was on the side table, close at hand. It was a thick book with a cloth cover apparently sewed on zealously by an amateur. The boy reached for it with an eagerness in his grasp that almost had affection in it. Then he propped the book up and opened it. Now he was a different boy. His face was alive, excited, his eyes full of delight as he turned the pages, flipping a stamp over here, caressing one there, pointing out his best specimens in a torrent of words.

"Now these, here's one of my best pages. I'm fairly strong here, see; I specialize pretty much in British colonies. Well, not entirely though. Here's Ceylon. This five rupee, that's worth six-fifty, that one is. It's worth more unused, though. I exchanged it for a USA Columbian with Terry Walters. His dad gives him lots of stamps. France. Now, I'm not so strong on France. There, see, Gold Coast, see? I only need two more to complete that set. The four shilling green, oh, boy, that's expensive, that is; costs six bucks. Leastways that's the list price in the Scott catalogue. You can often get 'em cheaper at auctions, though."

"Dean!" said his father.

"India. Yeah, I'm pretty fairly strong in the native states. Patiala. That one anna carmine is sure hard to get, plenty hard. I know a boy in Bayonne has the two anna; only he won't exchange, though. That's the way it is. Mauritius. One of the first countries to issue stamps. Didn't you know that? You didn't? Gee, I thought everyone knew that. You know the one penny head of Queen Victoria, their first? It's worth forty thousand bucks today. That's because it's scarce. I saw it once at a stamp exhibition in New York my dad took me to. See, I've got the six penny and the one shilling myself. That one shilling's a good specimen. I saved a long time to buy that, shoveled snow 'n'cut lawns 'n'everything. Malta. Not so good. But I'm improving. My uncle is buying me the five penny brown for my birthday. That's next Tuesday, the twenty-second. New Zealand. See, the five shilling Nile green. You might think it belonged in 1889, there. It doesn't, it's watermarked; it belongs where it is."

He unfastened the stamp and held it up to the light. All this meant nothing to Highpockets, who was mystified by the jargon. Then the boy licked the gummed sticker and pasted it back into the album with quick, expert movements.

"Dean, Dean! Please, Dean, don't bother Mr. McDade. He isn't interested in stamps."

This was untrue. Highpockets was slightly dizzy

from glancing much too quickly at pages flipped past his gaze, at rows and rows of colored stamps ranged in orderly lines in the album, bewildered by the flood of words, most of which meant nothing whatever to him. It was a language he couldn't speak. He was confused and also astonished at the change in the youngster. Certainly, he was interested.

Isn't this something! Here's a bigger nut than a baseball fan! All over stamps, too, imagine that! And next Tuesday, the twenty-second, is his birthday. Say, I must dig up some stamps for the kid. Wonder where you buy stamps, anyhow? If he wants stamps and likes stamps, I'll sure get him stamps. I sure will. Maybe some of these magazines will tell where to buy them.

He reached out and thumbed over the pile of magazines lying on the table. *Stamps. McKeel's Weekly. Scott's Monthly Journal. Harmer's Stamp Hints.*

"You take a lotta stamp magazines, don't you, Dean?"

"Yeah. Look! Looka here, Mr. McDade."

The ballplayer and the boy bent over the stamp album together, forgetting for just a few minutes that with an operation one never knows.

Chapter 12

Too early to tell, said Dr. Jansen over the telephone. Too early to tell, said his young assistant surgeon when Highpockets met him in the corridor of the hospital. Too early yet to tell much, said the nurses outside the door of the boy's room. That was the moment he realized the truth of the doctor's remark, that with an operation one never knew.

He's a strong kid, Highpockets kept saying to himself over and over. He's young, he's healthy, he has a circulation like the *New York Daily News*. But suppose things took a turn for the worse; suppose the boy actually had to lose a leg, so he could never run or play games again! All on account of a muffed fly ball and a dispute with a truck driver on a hot street in Brooklyn. If only I hadn't got mad and started off so fast that evening, he thought. Nope. I shouldn't feel that way about the accident. The whole thing just happened; it really wasn't my fault at all. The kid ran out and crashed into my car, and bang! I couldn't have helped what took place. Besides, I'm paying for the whole operation.

Only suppose it turns out badly! Suppose the kid has to lose a leg. Suppose the infection gets worse . . .

These were the thoughts he juggled in his brain as he lay awake night after night in the hot hotel room during the steaming weather at the end of July. He could visit the boy for only a few minutes at a time, but did not forget the stamps for his birthday. In spite of the pain in his leg—the doctors called it discomfort—the boy's face lit up when he saw the present, and grabbing at the package he pulled the stamps from the envelope.

Knowing nothing whatever about stamps or stamp collecting, Highpockets had bought the lot from a friendly clerk at Gimbel's, slightly astonished to discover that this was an expensive hobby. There they were, spread out on the bedsheet, sets of new, unused stamps with the numbers on, a fact which the clerk had explained made them more valuable. After one look, however, the face of the boy again dissolved into pain. The stamps in his hand dropped to the bed.

"Yeah, thanks lots. Thanks, Mr. McDade. Only now, see, I don't c'llect these. I don't c'llect this kind. I only c'llect up to 1900. I don't c'llect anything after 1900."

Highpockets wasn't sure what he meant by this,

yet he understood that the stamps somehow didn't fit into the boy's collection and were not what he wanted. Carefully placing them back in their envelope, the ballplayer slipped them into his pocket. Out in the corridor he wrote down what the youngster had said. "Don't collect after 1900."

Perhaps it was the strain of the pennant race, perhaps he was baseball-weary after the struggle of the spring and early summer. Perhaps it was worry over the boy's operation or just an inevitable mid-season slump. At any rate, something seemed to affect Highpockets' batting. There were days when it was impossible to get the ball away from the packed defense on the right side, when he couldn't get a shot to the outfield. Every night he went to bed saying to himself, Tomorrow I'll rip one. The next day his savage drives would go straight at the second baseman stationed in the hole where, with a normal setup, the hit would have meant a free passage into right field. He began to take third strikes with his bat on his shoulder, something he had never done in his whole baseball career. From .305 his batting average tumbled slowly to .300 and then nearer .290. Those home-run clouts were less frequent, he was breaking up fewer games with his grand slams. He fell into his slump, curiously enough, just when the rest of the club began to hit more powerfully.

The slump delighted the fans. As his hitting went off, they came out in greater numbers than ever to watch him stumble and give him a lusty razoo. "Let's get Highpockets' goat," they said, swarming into the stands with horns, cowbells, whistles, and powerful throats and lungs. To be sure, he was still drawing quite a few bases on balls. But, as Spike remarked to Jack MacManus, the club president, one morning when they were discussing the team's problem child, "You don't hit in runs with bases on balls."

MacManus observed the rookie's slump with concern, for the return of Roy Tucker from Johns Hopkins in Baltimore was still problematical. On weekdays when the crowd was not too large, the club president even tried to rope off several sections in deep right nearest Highpockets' position in the field. The fans caught on to this maneuver and increased their noisy heckling from a distance. They went after him all the harder, until he really had the miseries.

One afternoon in a tight game against the Cubs, he charged up to the edge of the boxes for a foul fly, the crowd roaring. The ball drifted gently with the wind into the first tier of boxes, just out of reach of the playing field. Highpockets came up to the box, reached over, got his glove on the ball, and then, stumbling among the scattering occupants in the seats, dropped it as he tumbled to the floor in a clatter of falling chairs.

He picked himself from the mess, the crowd yelling with delight from above.

"Highpockets, you're a bum in spades."

"Hey, McDade, you rockhead; you rockhead, McDade!"

"You louse you, Highpockets."

He was completely disgusted with himself for losing the ball and missing that important out which he felt ordinarily he would have made. On the mound Bones Hathaway stood watching, hands on his hips, yanking savagely at his cap as he turned to take a new ball from Jocko. Highpockets noticed this and was furious, annoyed with Bonesey, with himself, most of all with the howling mob of wolves in the stands. Over one shoulder he yelled at them as he walked back to his place in deep right.

"Aw, nuts to you guys, all of you!"

It was all the mob needed, those who heard him and those who did not. The entire right field stands rose, delighted to be able to needle him, their croakings and honkings resounding across the diamond. There were now runners on second and third, two down, and the Cub slugger at the plate. As usual, given another life, he slashed the next pitch, banging a line drive off the concrete in left field.

So instead of getting out of the traffic jam, Bonesey had a two-run deficit to face and a batter perched on second base.

He can't take it, said the fans, as his average continued to drop. He can't take it. Remember how everyone laughed when the Reds tried that swing-shift. Well, it's sure paid off. Lots of old-timers said the shift was silly, that it would never work against him as it had failed lots of times against other batters in the past; that he would soon learn to hit to the opposite field; that you can't get away with that sort of thing in the majors; that he was too smart a batter to be fooled by a packed defense.

It had worked far better than anyone could have imagined. Highpockets' batting miseries grew worse. Possibly he didn't have his entire mind on baseball. For after every contest he would race in to the clubhouse in his soaking clothes and rush to the telephone.

One afternoon that week it took longer than usual to get the number. The line was busy and Highpockets grew feverish with impatience. At last the connection was made. "Foxcroft nine, seven two hundred? Bushwick? Lemme have Miss Simpson, the head nurse on the sixth floor, please. Miss Simpson? Hit's Cecil McDade. How's the boy to-day? No change? Too early yet? I see; I understand, I getcha. How's his temperature? It is? That ain't so good, is it? I see. O.K. Tell him mebbe I'll drop in for a few minutes tonight. And look, tell him I'll bring some stamps, some new stamps along with me."

Then Highpockets slipped off his clothes and into the showers and so into his street clothes and out to grab a taxi, brushing away half a dozen kids who were pleading for his autograph. All the while thinking, Gee, he's just Henry Lee's age; same age, same grade in school. Imagine if Henry Lee lost his leg and couldn't drive the tractor or play ball or do anything round the place! Imagine that!

"Where ya wanna go, mister?" The taxi driver had one hand on the clock.

"New York. Scott Stamp and Coin Company. That's Fifth offa Forty-seventh."

Highpockets reached the place and went directly up to the clerk behind the counter.

"Could I see the manager, please?"

The clerk looked at him and was dubious. What did he want to sell?

"I ain't sellin' nothin'. I'd just like to learn something about stamps, that's all. See now, I just don't know a thing about stamps, and I'd like for to have the best expert in the place explain things to me, tutor me, kind of, say for a week, so I'd understand what this stamp collecting is all about."

The clerk's mouth opened. He'd never heard such an unusual request before. Highpockets continued: "Oh, I'd pay right good for the information. But I'd like to know all about stamps. For instance now, what's it mean when a feller doesn't collect after 1900?"

Highpockets had learned something. There's no easy way to a boy's heart. Like everything else, you have to work for it.

Chapter 13

IT was hardly what one would call a well-ordered hospital room, but then the boy had a wise and understanding nurse. In a basin of water on the table were floating bits of colored paper; other bits curled up on a huge piece of blotting paper. Beside him on the bed were the album, two catalogues, a watermark detector, a magnifying glass, a pair of tweezers, and a generous packet of stamp hinges.

The ballplayer and the boy bent over the stamp together. Then the youngster reached out, took a bottle off the little table beside the bed, let several drops of benzine fall onto the stamp which he held in his hand with the tweezers. Then he replaced the stopper in the bottle.

His hands trembled slightly as he did so.

"You cold?"

"Naw. I'm hot." He peered through the magnifying glass in Highpockets' hand. "Look, it's this one here, 1884, watermarked Crown and C.A. See?"

The ballplayer took the stamp in the tweezers

from the boy and held it to the light, looking at it awhile with attention. "Nope, I b'lieve you're dead wrong on that one, Dean. Yep, hit's 1886 not 1884, and hit's watermarked Crown and C.C. The cancellation on the other side hides that second letter. You hafta watch out. See, hit's a C, not an A. That makes a big diff."

"Aw, gee! The 1884 is worth fourteen bucks. This one is only worth two-fifty. It's always like that; you find yourself stuck with the cheaper stamp, always. Here, lemme see for myself. Yeah, guess you're right, though. It's a C, not an A. Shucks!"

He shivered again.

The nurse came into the room. She held a glass of water on a saucer in her hand. Two pills were on the saucer.

"Time for your medicine, Dean." She raised her eyebrows at Highpockets, who understood.

"Uhuh." He slipped off the side of the bed. "Guess mebbe I'd better shoot along."

"Aw, gee, no. Why don't you wait? You just came. We've only started on these stamps. Don't go now, please don't go now."

"You need your rest, Dean," said the nurse in nursy tones. "You must sleep, else you won't get well. Come on now; take these, please."

"You take yer pills, Dean. I must get moving. Have a mighty tough series coming up, a night

game and a double-header the day after, 'count
of that postponed game last month. That's wicked.
I need my rest too, same as you. I shore do." He
looked at the boy, whose eyes seemed bigger than
ever. Overnight he was a different kid. Perhaps it
was the haircut. His hair had been trimmed short
with a clipper. No blond mop waved around his
forehead now. His eyes seemed bigger. The haircut made a difference in his whole appearance, yet
his face was changed also, paler and grimmer.
"Y'see, I hafta get my rest same as you," explained
the ballplayer.

"Who you playin' tomorrow?"

"The Cards."

"Who's the Cards?"

"St. Louis."

"Oh," he said, sucking slowly on the water and
downing one pill with great effort. "Are the Cards
good? Do they have a good team?" He finally
swallowed the second pill, reluctant to have his
visitor depart, even willing to discuss baseball at
such a moment.

"I'll say. Just about the best. They head the
league at present; they're hotter'n a three-alarm
fire. O.K. then. I'll be over in the early afternoon
tomorrow. You be a good kid and sleep. An' do
what Miss Simpson tells ya, hear me!"

"Aw, gee. Just when we were getting things

done, too. You help me with my Western Australias, will ya? Please, Mr. McDade, before ya go, please . . ."

"No, Dean, your mother'll be in to see you later on."

"My mother's dead."

"Oh. I didn't know. Yer dad then."

"My dad! My dad! He doesn't like stamps. Please stay, Mr. McDade."

"Not tonight, son. We'll clean up your Western Australias and maybe the Falkland Islands tomorrow. You need your rest right now. And look, if you're good, if Miss Simpson tells me over the phone tomorrow the first thing that you've taken your shots and your medicine, and slept like a good boy, tell ya what. I'll bring ya that four penny puce, with the C.A. watermark on it. How's that!"

"Ya will! Ya will!" His face lit up, his expression changed, he was a different person. "Ya will? Promise?"

"Oh, no. I don't promise a thing. This is strictly up to you. You be a good boy and do as yer told, and you'll get it. Depends entirely on you, and what Miss Simpson reports to me tomorrow morning over the phone. Now then, I'll see you in the afternoon. G'd night now."

He left the hot room, followed closely by the nurse, the empty glass in one hand. "Mr. McDade, the doctor wants to speak to you a moment. He's in the staff office on the second floor. He asked me to have you stop past on your way out."

Highpockets went down in the elevator, got off at the second floor, and knocked on the doctor's door.

"Yes, come in, come in. Glad to see you, Mr. McDade. I had to look in and check on our patient this evening, and I thought perhaps you'd like to know how things were going. Sit down, please."

He fumbled nervously with some papers on his desk, lit a cigarette, fumbled and shuffled the papers some more. Then he swung round in his chair and faced Highpockets.

"Mr. McDade, the boy isn't coming along as fast as we'd hoped. Naturally, it's not possible to tell definitely, but probably the crisis in his case will come some time tomorrow or the next day. If the condition doesn't improve, then . . ."

"You mean . . . otherwise you'll have to amputate his leg?"

The electric fan on the bookcase buzzed and whirred. "It's something to be considered," said the doctor gravely.

Holy mackerel! If only I'd nabbed that fly ball; if only I'd kept my temper with that truck driver! If only . . . if only . . . if only . . .

"Mind you, I don't say it will be necessary. I

merely suggest it as a possibility. Much depends on these next couple of days, which is why I wanted to talk to you. If we can keep his spirits up when the crisis sets in, that will be a big asset. He seems to have taken a great fancy to you, Mr. McDade. I dare say you're one of his heroes."

"H'm . . . well, yessuh . . . that is . . . not exactly . . . yeah."

The doctor continued. "If only we can keep his spirits up. It's a sort of team, y'see, you and his family and the nurses and myself, all working together on him. You're a baseball player; you understand the importance of team play better than anyone. I can see that."

Yes, and I can see you don't know the first thing about the setup on this year's Dodgers, thought Highpockets. Well, anyhow . . .

"So if you'll hold yourself in readiness to drop in as much as possible during the crisis, I'm sure it will help. Mind you, I have every hope. I have hopes because he has such a strong constitution. Of course, in a thing of this sort you never know for sure; complications can set in. But we'll work together as a team. He's mighty fond of you because you're a ballplayer. I guess you're one of his heroes."

"Yeah . . . shore 'nuff . . . I see whatcha mean, Doctor. You can count on me."

One of his heroes, hey! Well . . .

Highpockets went into the steaming August evening in the big city. Hope he knows more about medicine than he does about baseball, that medic, thought the ballplayer. He stood hesitating in his fatigue between the humid subway and an inviting taxi parked at the curb. The driver leaned out to open the door.

"Taxi, sir?"

"Nope, that'll cost me two-fifty. I could get him that Grenada black surcharge, the half penny purple he wants so bad to complete his set. Only I'm tired, and that smelly subway's mighty darned hot these nights.

"Taxi, sir, taxi?"

"No, thanks," said Highpockets. He turned, walked round the corner, and on down to the subway.

Someone had left an evening newspaper in the seat in the empty car as he entered. He picked it up. The sheet was opened at Casey's column.

The Dodgers in fourth place are still a hustling, battling crew, and they come up to the start of their next to last western trip in a strategic spot to take advantage of any lapses on the part of the league leaders. Considering the injuries they've had the past month, with Jocko Klein in and out of the line-up on account of a split thumb, and the disaster to the Kid from Tomkinsville, their star gardener, they've done about all anyone could ask.

The worst handicap, besides the failure of some of their older pitchers to come through, has been the collapse of their much publicized rookie, Cecil "Highpockets" McDade, who threatened to tear the league apart with his bat all through last spring. When the Brooks took the blankets off the North Carolina lad at the start of the campaign, it seemed he was a cinch to batter Babe Ruth's home-run record into oblivion. But the big farm boy still hasn't learned to hit to the opposite field, and after whacking twenty-seven homers up to the 15th of July, has struck a bad slump. At last the pitchers seem to have found out his weakness. They've high-lowed him, pulled the string, fed him sliders and tricky knucklers and just about every freak throw in the book. The way to stop him is with soft stuff. He's seen so much of it that his timing is off, and he often stands there with his bat on his shoulder, looking like a typical number eight hitter when the ball whistles through the slot.

Yet the Dodgers can't be counted out of the race, for they're a dead game ballclub all the way. They still have a chance to cop, especially if they can wallop the Redbirds, who come in for a four-game series at Ebbets Field tomorrow. Given good pitching, they ought to make things interesting for the league leaders, and perhaps start that western trip in a position that makes them dangerous for the clubs above them in the standing. Spike Russell, their courageous pilot, hasn't given up on his outfit, and Spike has been in some tight spots before and come through. A lot depends on McDade.

Should the North Carolina boy start to hit as he did in the early part of the season, the Brooks are a good bet to win. Lately Highpockets has been sulking like a small boy over the defensive shifts thrown against him, yet he's done nothing to meet them. There's no secret that the lanky Southerner has never been the most popular man on the club, and the story is that he got into a rhubarb with one of the ace hurlers in the lockers not long ago. If he wants to begin hitting to left and become a team player, he'll discover a change in his mates' attitude over-night. This is strictly up to Highpockets.

He tossed the paper to the seat. He was hot all over and not from the heat. He glanced hastily up and down the car. At one end two young men were looking at him curiously, and he knew exactly what they were saying to each other.

"That's Highpockets McDade . . . that bum . . . that rockhead!"

Chapter 14

WHENEVER ballplayers have a night game ahead, they lie in bed as long as possible, trying to save up energy for the game to come. Rising simply means hours of sitting around hotel lobbies, of lounging in a hot bedroom reading the sports pages or the comics. So the longer they stay in bed, the more time they kill before the moment to leave for the park to dress. That day Manhattan was liquid with humidity. You were damp if you merely leaned over to pick up a newspaper off the floor, or if you sat still and did nothing. That's the kind of an August day it was.

Highpockets was a farm boy and he never needed an alarm clock to wake him up. No matter how late the game had lasted the previous evening, he invariably woke promptly at five-thirty each morning. By some persistence, he had trained himself to turn over and sleep a couple of hours longer. Not that day. At five-thirty he was wide awake. He lay in the sweltering room, thinking about his rise from the minors through Boise and Fort Worth, his batting slump, and Dean Kennedy and his accident, and stamps—yes, of course, stamps. He thought of all he had learned in the past weeks—cancellations and perforations and surcharges and imprints, Straits Settlements and Hong Kong and Rhodesia and places he never knew existed a month before. In school he had not realized the British had so many colonies. Now it was understandable why Dean got an A in "geogerfy."

Six, six-thirty, seven, and eight. He lay there wide awake. At last he rose, showered and shaved carefully, and went down to breakfast. He was not hungry. Even in the air-conditioned grill he found difficulty in eating eggs and bacon.

At ten he called the hospital. There was the usual delay in getting the nurse. A strange nurse came to the telephone. The report was indefinite and not good. She simply said that Dean's temperature was still up and rising, that he had been uncomfortable much of the night.

Uncomfortable! There's that word again, thought Highpockets.

He got the new red Ford from the garage and drove over to the stamp company, where he spent an hour with a clerk, looking over stamps. By this time he was a knowledgeable purchaser with a fair idea of the value of a stamp and its condition. He bought the four penny puce, watermarked C.A., and also a set of seven Falkland Islands from the one-half penny yellow green to the one shilling bistre brown, all unused and in perfect shape. Because they were a set he got them below catalogue prices, yet at a cost that seemed to him considerable. Once again it was forced upon him that stamp collecting was not an inexpensive hobby.

Miss Simpson's face was graver when he reached the hospital in the early afternoon. The boy was more hollow-eyed and paler than the previous day. If his appearance had changed, so had that of the room. Now it was a sickroom. Flowers were on the table where once the stamp album held a prominent place. On the little stand beside his bed, a thermometer was stuck in a glass of water. Over everything was the queer, unpleasant smell of infection, a smell that assailed Highpockets the moment he entered. Now the shades were half drawn. This room was different; it was a battlefield like a baseball diamond, and he felt it immediately.

Sick the boy might be, yet not too sick to enjoy his stamps. As he yanked them with trembling fingers from their envelope, his expression grew animated and keen.

"Gee! Gee! Falkland Islands! Gee, thanks. Thanks lots, Mr. McDade; thanks a whole lot. That's swell of you. And the four penny puce, oh, boy! Mint, too. Gee!"

"Where's your album, Dean?" He spoke without thinking, carelessly, and the second he spoke he knew he should never have mentioned the album. Glancing up into the eyes of the nurse he received a warning look.

"Aw, gee, my dad took it away from me last night. He's always taking my stamp album away." Dean's head fell back upon the pillow as a spasm of pain went through his leg. "Dad, he took it away. I'm gonna ask Dr. Jansen can I have it later on." He fingered the stamps, pushing each one up on its hinge, touching each bit of paper gently, excitement in his eyes.

Why, the kid loves stamps. He really loves them like I love pasting the ball over the right field fence, or that wonderful feel of the bat when you've caught a fast one on the noggin. He sure loves stamps, this kid, doesn't he? Maybe I understand why, now.

The boy fingered the stamps a long while. Then his hand, hot and dry, fell on that of the ballplayer by the edge of the bed. "Gee, thanks, Mr. McDade. You're swell. You like stamps, don'cha?" His head sank back once more on the pillow. His breathing became slower and more difficult. His eyes closed.

"Yeah . . . you're shore welcome, Dean, you

shore are. Well, mebbe I'd better be running along now, Nurse."

The clutch on his hand tightened instantly. The eyes of the boy opened. "Aw, don't go away; please don't leave yet. My dad, he took away my album, but he'll let me have it again. Dr. Jansen will. I'll ask him will he leave me have it."

"Yeah, by-and-by he will." Highpockets laid the small hand on the bed. It slipped from his grasp and dropped inertly to the sheet. "I gotta get me a rubdown and dress before batting practice. Night game this evening. We start batting practice early, y'know."

"Look! Will ya come back tonight after the game, will ya, please, Mr. McDade? Please. You can help me with my Falkland Islands. I'll let you stick 'em in."

"Sure, sure, I will if the Doc'll allow me. Effen he says O.K., I'll come back, I promise."

"All right now. You promised. G'd-by. Be sure and come back after the game."

Highpockets spoke to the nurse about it as he left. She telephoned the doctor at his office, and the doctor replied that perhaps if the boy really wanted Highpockets there, it would help to have him around. He could stay outside, in the corridor, in case the boy asked for him. So he agreed to return after the game.

It was a game he felt would never end, a long, an eternal struggle that lasted far into the hot August night. It was ten-thirty; it was eleven-thirty; it was nearly midnight before Bob Russell singled Highpockets home with the winning run after he had been passed in the last of the thirteenth.

Rushing into the clubhouse, he stepped out of his monkey suit, heavy with dirt and perspiration, and quickly into the showers. He was out and dressed when his teammates had hardly taken off their clothes. They watched as he raced for the door. Same old Highpockets, giving everyone a brush-off, can't even stop to say good night. What a guy!

Without pausing for a meal, he bought a hot dog and jumped into his car in the parking lot across the street. He drove quickly to the hospital, which he reached just before one o'clock. He had been awake since five-thirty; he was tired, beaten, drained, and empty when he got to the sixth floor, dark save for a night lamp on the desk of the nurse on duty. Up and down the corridor other nurses crept silently from various doors. He sat waiting for the lad's own nurse to come out. Finally she left the room and noticed him sitting beside the desk, waiting. "Been here long?" she asked. The doctors were having a consultation inside. He sat wiping his forehead, wondering whether he had time for a bite to eat, yet not daring to leave in case the boy should call for him. At last the two medicos emerged. Their faces were grave and drawn. Dr. Jansen came across to the desk.

"He's been asking for you all evening, so we're going to let you go in and sit there. Try to keep him from talking if you can."

From the grim attitude of the doctor Highpockets understood how serious it was, guessed that it was worse even than the loss of a leg. He was bewildered by the whole thing. The boy had been so healthy, so . . . so . . . all right the previous week.

He opened the door and entered. The kid's face, flushed and feverish, was on one side of the pillow. In his hand he clutched the stamps from the Falkland Islands. His breathing was rapid, abnormal. The nurse turned to Highpockets as he sat down. It was a new night nurse; she understood, she smiled faintly. He took his place in the stiff chair beside the bed. Dean opened his eyes.

" 'Lo," he said faintly. One hand stretched out, or rather waved feebly in the air. Highpockets reached across and took it, a small hand, white against his own big brown paw.

A luminous clock ticked away on the night table. Highpockets forgot his fatigue, forgot his hunger, forgot everything save the struggle of the boy in the bed. Then, in the armchair behind, he noticed the kid's father, dozing. Still the boy held on to the hand of the Dodger's right fielder with his hot grip. It was two o'clock, it was two-thirty, it was three. The man's arm ached, his fingers were wet and tired; he clung to that hot hand still.

Finally the nurse rose, felt of his pillow, went out for a fresh, dry one and returned. Highpockets dropped the hand. The boy stirred.

"Mr. McDade." The voice was cracked and hoarse. "Don't go. Please don't go."

"Why, no, Dean, I'm not leaving. I'm still here, see. I came back right after the game and I'm gonna stay."

"Take my Falkland Islands; you keep 'em for me, will ya, Mr. McDade?"

From under the bedclothes came his other hand clutching still the crumpled envelope with the stamps in it. "Sure, I'll take 'em; I'll take care of 'em for you, Dean. Don't you worry, I'll take good care of 'em."

The boy sank back exhausted onto the fresh pillow which the nurse shoved under him. The father stepped into the corridor for a cigarette, and Highpockets followed to inquire about the boy's condition. To his surprise, the worried man seized him by the arm.

"How d'ya do it? How d'ya do it, huh?"

Highpockets was puzzled. Do what?

"How d'ya do it? Sometimes I can't cope with that-there kid. Seems like he gets away from me, somehow. I aim to be a good father and all that, yet one way or another, I don't understand, he wants you here tonight. How d'ya do it?"

Highpockets was puzzled still. It was the anxious look of the father who suddenly sees he hasn't been a success with his boy. Yet how *did* he do it? Why did the youngster want him there that evening? Highpockets couldn't exactly explain. He only knew one thing; it sure wasn't sport they had in common, the two of them.

The nurse passed them in the hall. Highpockets tiptoed back to his chair in the room. He took the feverish hand of the boy. Now he was all alone with the restless figure in the bed. He realized now that he, too, was exhausted, weak and weary so he could hardly sit up straight. Yet nothing counted, nothing was real save the boy, prisoner of his illness there in the dim room. No, nothing, not the Babe's home-run record, waiting to be broken, not even the farm at home, and the education of his brothers and sisters. He glanced anxiously at the swollen face on the pillow.

Then the queer breathing set in once more, a sort of change of breathing during which Dean's hand tightened in agony over the fingers of the ball-player. The spasm grew worse, subsided slowly after a while, then died away. The nurse leaned down and wiped the boy's cheeks and forehead with a damp towel. He seemed almost gone; he was a gaunt shadow on the white pillow, a skeleton. Yet his grip was as fierce as ever on the ballplayer's hand. Now Highpockets knew what it was—the will to live. This was it.

The clock showed four-fifteen. Four-twenty. Four-thirty. Already, through the edges of the curtains, a faint, dim grayness, delicate, imperceptible, was nevertheless there in the sky. The boy stirred, opened his eyes.

"Don't go away. Don't go away . . ."

"No, Dean, I'm here. I shan't leave. Don't you worry, I won't go away."

"Mr. McDade." He whispered again. "Mr. Mc-Dade."

The fingers tightened around the ballplayer's hand. "Hit's O.K., big boy. Hit's O.K. I'm still here."

Chapter 15

OF all that long afternoon with its scorching heat and its fierce struggle between two good ballclubs, each of whom refused to admit the other was good, he remembered little. Sitting later that evening in the hot room, listening once more to the strained breathing of the boy and watching his fight for life, even those two important games, even his own place in the thing called baseball, seemed not very vital. Because the kid on the bed might be Henry Lee; that's the way Henry Lee would look if his hair was cut and he was sick and weak and ill.

What he recalled of that double-header afterward was the exhausted feeling he had as he drew on the trousers of his monkey suit before the first game, and then the dragged-outness in his bones as he shagged the long flies at practice. And later on, in the game, when one can forget one's troubles in the team sorrows, came the procession of Dodger pitchers taking an early walk—Razzle and Homer Slawson and Jerry Fielding and the new youngster,

Chris Terry, one after the other, stepping confidently to the mound, and then off again. He remembered also the long-ball hitter of the Cards,
and how he looked at the plate in that awkward
batting stance, and the way the ball went sailing
over his head into Bedford Avenue, and the yells
and jeers of the mob. And the next batter. And the
next. And the next.

You know how it is with hitters; one man does
it, and the next man catches the fever and steps in
and clouts one, and so on and so on all down the
line. Even the bottom of the batting order. Everyone smashing them into the slot; a run, another
run, another and another. Dismay! Disaster! The
dissolution of a team.

Highpockets stood there motionless and helpless
in the burning sunshine, watching the pitchers
shuffle out of the bullpen, and the strange, hurt
way the previous man stumbled off the mound,
touching the peak of his cap, slapping his glove
nervously against his thigh, wiping his hand across
his shirt front. Then the desultory handclaps as he
came toward the dugout and vanished underneath
the passageway to the clubhouse. Spike stood out
there beside the rubber, hands on hips, waiting for
each hurler to amble in from deep right field. Jocko,
his mask on, scuffed up the dirt with his spikes,

while the crowd roared from above and around them as the runs mounted on the scoreboard.

103 042 61
000 000 00

All the while Highpockets stood there helpless in the burning sun, watching the crumbling of a team.

He recalled later that in the clubhouse, while the team ripped off their soaking wet clothes and changed into fresh uniforms between games, the reporters pestered him with the usual questions.

"Nope, guess not. I looked at a lot of good pitches, that's all. I say I looked at them and just didn't hit. Shucks, he made me hit *his* pitch, not mine. His delivery is shore rough; he's a wheel man, has the ball way back here. Not one of his balls is fat. Well, that's how it is. S'cuse me, will ya, please, fellas? I gotta make an important phone call."

He walked away, as the sportswriters looked at each other. Even the players glanced over curiously. "So that's it, that's what's biting him," said one of them. "Must be a girl has Highpockets down, him going six for nothing this way. Must be his girl has chucked him over."

The lines to the hospital were all busy. He was afraid he would never get the connection in time. One by one, in twos and threes, he saw the team leave, heard them tramp out and the click-click,

click-click of their spikes and the door slamming. A warning that game time was fast approaching. Now hardly anyone was left in the big room. Just Chiselbeak picking up their wet clothes, and the Doc in the corner working over one of the pitchers on the rubbing table. Then the door banged again, and someone returned for his glove or a pet bat or a new pair of sun glasses. Still the hospital number was busy; it took forever to reach, and when he finally did get it, the time seemed endless before he could get the sixth floor and Miss Simpson.

At last her voice came. It was—for her—excited. The boy's temperature was going down at last.

"He's better this afternoon," she said. "He's really better for the first time in a fortnight. The doctors are pleased."

He's better at last. He's better, thought High-pockets, as he went through the runway to the field where the game was about to begin, the two managers strolling up to the umpires with the line-ups in their hands. The two pitchers were tossing in their last warm-ups. Spike Russell came along the bench, an anxious look on his face.

"Take it easy, take it easy this time, big boy; you just take it easy a while. Alan's going in at right."

Highpockets stood motionless. Alan Whitehouse in my spot! Why, that's the first game I haven't started since April sixteenth, the very first one!

His face flushed. So I'm benched, he thought. Rage and humiliation filled him, for he was a ballplayer first of all, and real ballplayers want to play ball. Then slowly the remembrance of the telephone call came over him; he sank back and slumped to the bench. Aw, what's the difference? The kid's better, the kid'll pull through now. That's what really counts.

The public address system was sounding off with the line-ups, as the Dodgers trotted out on the diamond.

"Whitehouse, number six, right . . ."

Hey, Whitehouse in right field! Not that mug who doesn't like Brooklyn; Highpockets is out. A great hoot filled the ballpark, grew louder still and louder, bounced back against the stands in left center and echoed from behind the plate. Highpockets sat slumped on the bench with old Fat Stuff and the substitutes and one or two pitchers who were not on bullpen duty, listening as the roar from the mob increased in volume, until the whole packed throng was giving him the grand razoo. He sat there, and for once it didn't really matter; it didn't annoy him; he just didn't care. After all, the kid's better, isn't he?

Chapter 16

ONCE Fat Stuff was young, a star and a starting pitcher for the Dodgers. Years went past and at last the managers had to use him more sparingly. Spike Russell still got plenty of work from him as a relief hurler, and the boys always said Fat Stuff spent so much time in the bullpen he got his mail there. An ancient gag, yet one sure to trace a smile on the pitcher's lined face. Finally the moment arrived when there were little bulges of flesh over his hips, and a fold of fat beneath his chin. Fat Stuff then became most useful as a coach, helping the new men on the pitching staff and passing along his vast knowledge of players and the game to the youngsters on the Brooklyn squad. For he had as shrewd a judgment of baseball as anyone on the club, yes, even including Charlie Draper, the third-base coach who had been around the league for twenty-five years.

The Dodgers were on the road and were playing Chicago that afternoon. Highpockets, still benched,

136

sat in the dugout beside Fat Stuff. The oldster squinted through the glare at the Cub hurler astride the rubber. "Don't for the life of me understand why you fellas can't hit him. He's not fast enough to get by without a curve ball and, doggone, he hasn't got a curve."

"No curve, hey? His breaking stuff ain't so bad, Fat Stuff. Seems plenty like a curve when you're in there facing it. Why, he's won a lot of games for hisself this summer."

"Yeah, he has at that. Only I swear he hasn't got no curve. Maybe he jinxed you guys. Hullo, there's another pass."

With two out, the pitcher slowed to a walk, to a couple of walks that placed Brooklyn runners on first and second. Alan Whitehouse stepped in. Some perfunctory applause from the stands; no hooting, no jeering.

Alan struck the first pitch, topping a bounding roller just to the left of first. The first baseman tore in as the pitcher ran over to cover the bag, turned, and then threw to the base. It was a close race. Alan made a desperate slide as he neared the bag, and from the dugout seemed clearly to have the pitcher beaten.

But the umpire waved him out.

Instantly the whole Brooklyn bench was on its feet, yowling. Alan picked himself from the dust and charged toward old Stubblebeard, the umpire, tense with emotion. Red Cassidy, the first-base coach, was at his elbow. Spike Russell also raced from the dugout to protest the decision, while the stands yelled and the Brooklyn baserunners who had advanced on the play stood panting over second and third.

The three Brooklyn players surrounded the oldster in blue, angrily jawing. He folded his arms, set his chin and, turning, walked away with dignity in his steps. They followed with less dignity in theirs, still yapping like dogs for their dinner.

At last the old man turned. "Go back to the dugout, you fellas. Go back to that bench and button yer lip."

However, they stood there, hovering around him, still growling and arguing. At last the crowd got unruly and began to shout for the game to proceed. Finally the umpire signaled impatiently to resume play; Spike moved slowly back toward the bench, while Red Cassidy, shaking his head, returned to the coaching box back of first. Only Alan stayed on the diamond, chin to chin with the umpire. At last, smacking the dirt from his pants, he moved away with a parting thrust.

"Hey, there, fellas, what say we all chip in and buy the old geezer a Seeing Eye Dog?"

It was the "old" that did it. Stubblebeard had

been around a long while and been called names plenty of times; but the insinuation that he was past his prime hurt. He took one step forward. His right arm went up. His index finger pointed remorselessly toward the dugout.

"You there, number six, go take a shower fer yerself and be quick about it."

The crowd howled as Alan, still tossing remarks over one shoulder, sauntered deliberately into the dugout and disappeared from view. So, as they took the field again, the Dodgers were short a right fielder, and Highpockets at a sign from Spike picked up his glove, stepped from the bench, and loped into right field, adjusting his sun glasses around the back of his cap. The fans in the bleachers in right center rose as he approached. Then the gang in the right field stands took up the cry, louder and louder; groans and jeers sounded as he turned to face the plate, thumping his glove.

"Hey, there, Highpockets, you bum, you . . ."

"Oh, dogface, oh, Highpockets, you . . ."

He stood motionless, giving them nothing, never moving while abuse poured on him from every part of the big park. They kept at it until the first Cub hitter whiffed on three of Bonesey's shoots and then the noise died suddenly away. Yet they were on Highpockets more or less throughout the entire game.

He had no chances in the field, struck out in the fourth to the delight of the fans, and in the seventh came to bat with one out and Young and Swanny on second and first. The game was a scoreless tie, and a single meant a run, a big run. A homer, one of Highpockets' specialties, would sew it up.

Spike jumped from the dugout, went up to him in the circle, and whispered in his ear. Highpockets nodded as the infield slipped around into their customary defensive setup, and the fans yowled with pleasure. He strode to the plate, lugging the two bats, and tossed the leaded one to the side; then, smoothing the spike wounds made by the previous hitters in the dirt of the box, he stepped in.

The Chicago pitcher was tiring. His fast ball was not rising; his curve or what passed for a curve started to hang in there. Highpockets had noticed this from the bench the inning before; now it was apparent enough. Three hundred and fifty feet away was the low right field wall, and a lift over the fence would put the game on ice. The temptation to lean into the ball and bang one of those slants was terribly strong.

It was stronger still when the first pitch came across and he took it amid the jeers from the mob. The next was high inside, forcing him back. The third was a perfect ball on which to level off, a fast ball, waist high, one that he invariably crashed to deep right. Instead he obeyed orders. Taking two steps forward, he laid down a perfect bunt toward third base, just inside the foul line. The third baseman was on his heels, the pitcher asleep in the box.

The infielder rushed in, scooped up the ball, and threw too quickly. It bounced into the dirt after Highpockets had crossed the bag. The first sacker half stopped the throw which rose in the air behind him. He turned, searching for it, and before he recovered the ball Lester was over with the first tally of the game.

Swanny scored later on Spike's stinging single to center, and the Dodgers reached the ninth a couple of runs to the good. The Cub lead-off man in their half hoisted one of Bonesey's fast balls into the left field bleachers for the first Chicago run. The next batter worked a pass, and another hurler rose to join the two men throwing in the Brooklyn bullpen in right.

With all his skill and cunning, with all his patience, Bonesey went to work. The count on the batter reached three and two. Then he hit a ball into foul territory between third base and left field. The three men raced over; but it was Spike who took it for the first out of the inning.

The next batter was dangerous, with the tieing run still on first. He stood waiting for the fat pitch, fouling off ball after ball that kicked into the stands.

Finally he caught one squarely and laced it just over Lester Young's mitt on first. Highpockets was off. Charging in fast, he neared the sinking liner and made a desperate forward dive. Reaching out, he speared it with his glove and tumbled to the ground.

Up he came. Instead of holding the ball aloft for the whole ballpark to see, he immediately recovered balance, yanked back his arm, and fired on a line to Spike over second to prevent the baserunner from taking any liberties. Spike caught the ball as the Chicago player slid frantically back to first. Two out and the tieing run still on the sacks.

The manager slapped the ball several times in his glove, looked toward the bullpen to see that his relief men were throwing hard, and walked slowly over toward the mound, while the stands applauded Highpockets for his stab in the field. By golly, thought Spike, this time the boy means business. Now he's strictly business, the manager said to himself as he handed the ball to his pitcher in the box. The next man popped up and the game was over.

Seated at a desk in the club car of the *American* en route to St. Louis that night after dinner, Highpockets was catching up on his correspondence. The first letter was to his mother at home. The second to a boy in Brooklyn.

Dear Dean,

Mighty happy to have good news about you this afternoon and know you are getting ahead. That's swell. Now, you do whatever Miss Simpson tells you, and before the club gets home you'll sure be out of the hospital. We sure had a hot one today, tough game which we copped two to one. The pitchers are holding up just fine. I didn't start this afternoon but managed to bust into the line-up, and caught a hard one in the ninth, and helped bring the winning run across.

Hold on, now. That don't say a thing to that kid. Why, he won't have any idea what I'm a-driving at. He's not interested in baseball; he likes stamps. Funny, his living in Brooklyn like that and not being hot about baseball. Well, that's how things are. Let's see . . .

He took the letter in his hand and read what he had written, read it with care. There he sat, holding the sheet, examining the words critically. Then he tore it into four pieces. They dropped to the floor. He took up a fresh sheet of writing paper.

Dear Dean,

Mighty glad to have good news of you this afternoon and know you are making real progress. That's swell news. Be sure and do whatever Miss Simpson says, and you'll be up and out of the hospital when the club gets back to Brooklyn.

I intend to look real hard on this trip for that Gibraltar, the one penny rose you mentioned last time I was in to see you, for I know just how bad you need it to complete that page. We must find it somehow. Next week we move on to Cincinnati where they tell me there's a very good stamp dealer, and I hope to pick it up there. If not, in Chicago, at Marshall Fields, a big department store that has a first class stamp section. Think I told you about the Tasmanian Queen Victoria I snagged at that auction. That sure was a find. Now, you be sure and do what Miss Simpson tells you. . . .

Raz Nugent came into the car and leaned over his desk. "Hi there, big fella, still writing? Seems to me like you're writing letters all the time. Whatcha got, some dame back there in Brooklyn?"

Chapter 17

His teammates, being closest to him, naturally noticed the change first of all. And first of them to notice it was keen-eyed old Fat Stuff, the coach; then Spike Russell; finally the entire club was talking about Highpockets behind his back.

"What on earth has happened to the guy?" they asked each other. "Something has changed him," they agreed, as they discussed their teammate at meals or watched him from the bench while he took his raps. "Something or somebody has rocked old Highpockets for fair; he ain't the same busher he once was. Why, he's not a loner any more; he's really playing for the team now." They kidded behind his back, too, about his girl in Brooklyn and how he had become a different person. Almost human, at times, they said.

The fans across the circuit observed the change also. In the bleachers in right field in St. Loo, in the upper stands in Pittsburgh, in the jury box in Boston, under the scoreboard in deep center in

Wrigley Field where the Babe once parked his homers, folks who really knew the game turned to their neighbors. "Looka that-there Highpockets," they said, as he suddenly began to slash sizzling grasscutters into the hole where the shortstop ordinarily played. "Looka that guy, will ya! What's happened to him?"

The pitchers all over the league noticed it soon, too. "Say, what's cooking with this McDade of the Dodgers?" they asked each other. "He usta be a pushover for that defensive shift in right. Now he's no cinch to bang the ball straight into right field. What's cooking with him? You never know what he'll do nowadays; must be he's getting foxy all of a sudden. What say, Skip, maybe we just better change that shift on Highpockets today?"

The Dodgers did better as they went through the West. Little by little they improved their standing, picking up a game here and a game there, until they returned in third place by a couple of percentage points, the highest they had been since April.

Dean Kennedy was still in the hospital when the club returned to New York and, as it was an open date, Highpockets went to see him immediately after lunch. The youngster was alone in his room, working as usual on his stamps, the big album spread upon his lap. He looked up.

"Gee, Mr. McDade, I've been waiting for you and waiting for you all day long."

The face was rounder and fuller now, and there was a smile and a warming look of welcome on it that made the ballplayer warm also. He shuffled over and ran his long fingers through the kid's hair, the hair which had grown and was again falling down over his forehead. Like Henry Lee's hair, it was uncombed. Boys never comb their hair; why on earth should they?

"Gee, Mr. McDade, I'm awful glad you're back again. I've been waiting for you so long."

"Train was late, Dean. Seems there was a hotbox up near Syracuse that delayed us. We never got into Grand Central until just before noon, and I came over soon's I had my feed. How you feeling, son?"

"Me? Swell. I'm going home tomorrow. They promised me I could go home tomorrow. Look, now you can help me with my stamps, can't you?"

"You betcha, Dean. I've got the whole day. We're off this afternoon, you know, an open date. And I've got something for you, yessuh, I shore have. Found the one penny rose, that Gibraltar you needed. Well, I picked it up in an auction in Cincinnati like I told you I would if I could." He opened the suitcase on the chair, and rummaged in the cover. Finally he discovered the package of stamps inside. The eyes of the boy were dancing. "Here y'are, son."

Dean opened the packet carefully. "Gee! The one penny rose! I didn't hardly expect you'd ever get that one. Oh, boy! And this set . . . Say, that's really something." He fingered them with reverence, turning each stamp gently back on its hinges, looking it over with attention, examining it closely, like the expert he was. Condition? Good. Gum? Excellent. Perforation? Even. Cancellation? Light. "Gee! Thanks, Mr. McDade, you're swell to me. Thanks a whole lot. I guess that about fills my Gibraltar page. This sure makes me look good, doesn't it? I've got about the best Gibraltars of any of the gang now."

They worked over the album together, inspecting the new stamps with care, pasting them away slowly in the empty spaces in the book, lining up the St. Lucia, 1889, set, tasting the pleasure only a collector knows over a sudden and unexpected find.

Then all at once the boy closed the volume with a snap. He ran his fingers through his hair.

"Y'know what? I wish I could work on my stamps alla time. I sure do. Wish I didn't have to go back to school next month. Look, Mr. McDade, is it true that Washington didn't do so good in school when he was a boy?"

Highpockets was astonished. He hesitated. Say,

what's all this? Washington in school! How do I know what Washington did when he was a boy in school? We never learned that in history class, that I remember.

"Well, now, Dean, I really wouldn't know for sure about that, I really wouldn't. But Edison, he didn't do so well. I know he didn't do so good, and look at him. Just see what happened to Edison. So don't you let it get you down, boy, even if you don't like it. Stick in there. See now, you hafta go to school; everyone has to, y'know."

"Why?"

Yes, why? Why do kids have to go to school? To keep them busy, to keep them out of their mother's way at home? Or to get an education? If so, what is an education? What does that mean? Highpockets was puzzled as he sat on the edge of the bed, looking at the wide-eyed boy who asked such difficult questions. If the kid didn't get by at school, it surely wasn't because he was stupid. Then whose fault was it? The ballplayer sat there biting his lip, remembering that this was a question he had often asked himself, especially in high school when he wanted to be outdoors in the Carolina spring sunshine, practicing with the baseball team. Why do boys and girls have to go to school? He felt differently about school now, yet once he felt just as this boy felt today. How could it be explained? How can I say it so this youngster will understand.

"I guess it's something like this, Dean. School, well, it sort of teaches you to use your bean. It teaches you to think. No matter what you do later on, see, effen you was to be a stamp dealer, you gotta be sharp, you gotta learn how to think."

The boy's nose wrinkled. He was unconvinced. "Yeah. I don't want to go back to school next month. I hate it. Look. Mr. McDade, *you* don't have to think. You're a ballplayer. All you hafta do is hit home runs."

That struck home, and Highpockets was excited. He rose and walked up and down the room, concentrating upon this problem, feeling that perhaps he had the answer at last. The answer to a problem that was now unimportant to him, but that had once been terribly important, and was now to this youngster who wanted to work with his stamps instead of studying English and history and algebra. That's really it; the purpose of a school is to teach you to think. Some time he ought to say all these things to Henry Lee, the lazy little rascal who was always outdoors playing ball in the long spring evenings instead of doing his home work under the living room light.

"Boy, you was never so wrong in your life. One thing a ballplayer has to do is think, think every scc, alla time. Now when I'm a-hittin' in there, I'm tryin' to outguess that pitcher, and he, why, he's tryin' to do the same doggone thing. See now, it's his brain against mine. Then in the field, too, just the same, you must be thinking every single moment. Ever hear of Babe Ruth? You didn't? You did? Good! Well, now, there was a gent in baseball for twenty years more or less, and never once threw to the wrong base. Not once."

He could see the boy hadn't the slightest idea of what he meant. So he grabbed a sheet of paper from the table and drew a baseball diamond on it. "Here, lemme explain what I'm a-sayin'. See, here's first . . . second . . . third base. Here's home plate. Get it? O.K. Now then, from home to first, from here to here, is ninety feet; that's thirty yards; that's about one third the length of a football gridiron. O.K. It takes a speedy man in baseball clothes a little over three seconds to cover that ninety feet. Happen you've got a fast runner on base, on first, and the batter smacks a line single out your way into right field. Then what? Will the man on first try to stretch it? Will he go for third? Will he run from here, see, to here? Shall you throw to third base to cut him off? If so, and your throw is the least bit wild or gets away, he'll be safe; and what's more, the batter will probably grab off an extra base and come safely into second."

Dean was interested. "I see. Then you'd throw to second first-off."

"Wait a minute. Hold on now. It all depends. If the man on first tries for third and makes it safe, he'll be able to come home on a deep fly, and effen the score is tied, that's mighty important, that one run. But suppose there's two outs, he can't score on a fly to the outfield. So most likely he won't try to take that extra base; he won't risk it, especially when the game is close. You hafta think of this runner on first, and how fast he is, and how many bases he has stolen all year, and what the chances are of his taking off for third. Then you must judge how the wind is blowing, the speed of the ball that's hit your way, and how it bounces on the grass. You gotta make all these calculations—the speed of the runner, the number of outs, the lead the man had on first, the wind that's blowing sharp in your face; you must calculate all this in three seconds. Look, see here. Just get it on my watch . . . one . . . two . . . three. That's all the time you have. And that darn ball a-zippin' toward you on the turf, and the fans a-yellin' and a-screamin' at you . . ."

"Gee! I didn't realize baseball was like that! It's sure complicated, isn't it? The way stamps are, when you get deep down. How d'you ever remember it all? Don't you ever forget?"

"Boy, you better not forget. You better make the

right guess; you better throw to the right base. 'Cause you won't make the wrong throw many times. Effen you *do*, you'll find yourself down in Roanoke, pretty darn quick, too. See, Dean, y'understand now? Get it? In baseball like in everything else, you gotta think. That's what school does for you, it teaches you to think."

Highpockets had never reasoned this way before but, after all, wasn't that the real purpose of an education? You got it, you got it somehow; you got it either in school where it was easy to get, or else you got it the hard way, coming up through the minors, from Rocky Point to Boise to Fort Worth, where you learned by experience, by making mistakes and having to pay for them, by throwing to the wrong base and getting cuffed around afterward by the manager. But get it you did, one way or another.

He glanced over at the kid, who had a strange, far-off look on his round face. His big blue eyes were staring into space and he was paying no attention to those last sentences. Highpockets was slightly annoyed. Thinking about those darn stamps, most likely.

"Mr. McDade, will you do something for me? Will ya, please? Please, will ya?"

Now what? Now what's he want? That two buck orange and black of the Mississippi River Bridge to complete his Trans-Mississippi set, probably. That'll cost me plenty, that one will. Or perhaps he wants the 1897 Jubilee issue, to finish up that Canadian page. Shoot, I might as well say yes, if he really wants 'em. Stamps are an investment, they all tell you.

"Yeah, I will. Whatcha want, Dean?"

"You promise, will ya? When I get outa here tomorrow, I'd like for you to take me to a ballgame. One you're playin' in, Mr. McDade."

Chapter 18

EARLY September, autumn in the night air, the days still hot and the pennant race the same, as the Dodgers took over second place and climbed slowly toward the league-leading Cards. It was a different gang of ballplayers, and this was evident in many ways. Even the sportswriters who traveled with the club were cheerful, always an excellent indication of the team's morale.

Roy Tucker came into the clubhouse as they were dressing for the game, that wide grin on his face as usual. The room suddenly erupted into motion. In a second they were converging upon him, crowding around, slapping him on the back, shouting words of welcome. The Kid from Tomkinsville was needed on the squad both as a player and a friend.

Highpockets, lacing his shoes before his locker, listened to their tones, noticed the affection on their faces, saw Roy's evident delight at being with them once more, his pleasure at returning to the club after his long stay in the hospital.

Why can't I be like him? thought Highpockets. He loves folks and folks love him. See, they're grabbing his hand as if they meant it, and they really do. They want him back, they want him out there in center again; they need him badly these last days of the season. Only it's more than that. They wouldn't be that way over Paul Roth or Shiells, no matter how good they were. They sure wouldn't be that way about me. He's different; they missed him, we all missed him. Yes, doggone, I missed him, too.

Then Roy sauntered across the room. He spotted Highpockets over by his locker.

To his own surprise, the rookie, who had finished tieing his shoes and was standing up, suddenly found himself moving toward the Kid from Tomkinsville with outstretched hand.

"Mighty glad to have you back again, Roy. I shore missed you out there next door. Boy, we can use you right now, with those Cards coming next week."

Roy's grip was firm and friendly, and there was the same warm grin as he answered. "Miss me? D'ja really? That's good; that's fine. But I dunno, you kids seem to be doin' O.K. without me. Le's see now, Highpockets. Yesterday was your twenty-eighth, wasn't it? Twenty-eight straight games you've hit safely. Why, boy, you got a chance for DiMag's record."

"Shucks, Roy, that don't mean a darn thing; you know how 'tis."

He leaned, picked up his jacket, and moved toward the door. Only, hang it all, hitting in twenty-eight straight games does mean something, and nobody knows it better than Roy Tucker. He must have been following the club pretty carefully all the time he was in the hospital. Some guy, Roy is.

By this time the fans were coming out as much to see Highpockets hit safely in each game as to watch the Dodgers overtake the Cards. Sometimes he'd be passed a couple of times and only have two official at-bats. The crowd would watch in silence as he came down to his last raps toward the end of the game, and would rise cheering when he made a hit and kept his record alive. Each day the tension increased, the drama grew; each time he walked to the plate was an occasion.

The game that afternoon at the Polo Grounds was close and hard-fought all the way through. The only score came in the sixth, when Highpockets stepped in, and, as usual, the opposing infield shifted to the right for him. The shift was the same; so was the pitching, which was close to his fists as before. That day it was even closer than ever. The second pitch dusted him off and he fell backward from the plate, sprawling awkwardly in the batter's box.

Highpockets rose, slapping his pants and rubbing off his hands amid cries from the stands, annoyed and angry, his face flushed. The next ball was a low, down-around-the-knees curve, and he tommy-hawked it. That ball went on a line straight for the stands in right field, a homer from the moment it left his bat. Landing in the sixth row of the lower seats, four hundred and fifty feet from home plate, it knocked in the crown of a man's straw hat, while Highpockets circled the bases before the yowling thousands. Only this time the din had in it more approval than derision; this time it was in a very different key from the sounds he had been accustomed to hear early in the season.

Charlie Draper was waving his arms behind third as he passed, and the photographers were lined up on the first-base side of the plate, waiting for him as he came in. Others were there, too; Jocko, certainly Jocko was always there, not only because he followed Highpockets in the batting order, but because Jocko was Jocko. Only this time Jocko wasn't alone. Spike and Roy Tucker, in uniform for the first time, and Bob Russell and Red Cassidy from the coaching box back of first, and Fat Stuff off the bench, they all came toward him as he neared home. He felt their bodies jostling his, the friendly contact of hips and thighs when he came across the plate, their hot paws extended to him, someone grasping his right hand, someone else his left. It was a traffic jam around the batter's box. How different from the first of the year, he thought, as together they all trotted back to the bench. Now he was one of them, now he was part of the team.

That was the only score of the game, the only hit he made all afternoon, and the twenty-ninth game in which he had batted safely. He came up once more, to face the same ugly look on the face of the pitcher, the same fast balls dangerously close to his body, all but dusting him off again. He took two pitches inside and fouled a couple of balls upstairs. Then came a slider right at his head.

He turned, spun round, instinctively threw up his arm to protect himself. The ball struck him squarely on the outer point of his elbow. His bat clattered to the ground as he stood wringing his arm in pain.

Spike Russell was by his side like a shot, while Draper raced in from third and Steamboat Jackson, the plate umpire, stood by watching, a frown on his face. The blow hurt. Highpockets' face was twisted in pain as Spike hastily massaged his elbow. Finally he walked down toward first. There was deep silence over the field.

The elbow hurt badly for a while, but he forgot it in the excitement of the next inning. In the last of the ninth, the Giants began to tee off on Chris Terry, the Dodger rookie. The first man beat out an infield roller. The second slashed a terrific drive to Paul Roth in deep left, who made a wonderful catch up against the concrete, almost into the visiting bullpen. The baserunner on first slid safely into second on the out.

One out, a man on second, the winning run at the plate. Burns, the Giant catcher, stepped up, while in right the Brooklyn bullpen went into action, Raz and Homer Slawson furiously working. Now the stands rose, yelling, screaming, clapping hands in unison to unsettle the young Dodger pitcher. It was a tight moment.

The batter was a man to whom you had to pitch. He fouled them off, one after the other, until on the three and two count he got hold of a curve and drove a hard-hit ball to deep right. Highpockets yanked down his sun glasses. Even in the excitement of the play he noticed that sudden, sharp pain in his elbow.

Back he went, back, sighting the ball as he ran, back until he almost reached the fence. He was nearing it, he was close, he felt the wall behind him when the ball descended. Raising his hands high above his head and leaning against the boards, he managed to haul down the drive for the second out. His whole arm hurt as he rifled the ball to the infield while the runner galloped into third. Now there were two out, the tieing run on third base, and the winning run at the plate.

Bob Russell took the throw and relayed it to his brother. Spike walked in, rubbing the ball up in his hands, to the perspiring pitcher on the mound. One tremendous whack to left, another to right. Should he stick with this rookie or call for help from the bullpen?

"Here, Chris, lemme hold this for you; it's plenty hot. I'll just cool it off for you a while." He stood for a minute, talking quietly to the youngster. "Look, Chris, come down overhand. Stride toward the spot you're throwing at, and the ball will go in there for you." Then he handed over the pill.

The youngster grinned and stepped back on the slab, checking the runner on third. He wound up quickly and whipped a fast ball under the batter's club. Then another strike, an inside curve which the man swung at and missed. And a third in succession. The game was over.

Loose, free, and happy, the gang poured from the dugout and tramped across the field to the clubhouse in deep center. They were laughing and joking as they piled up the stairs, hot, panting, and relaxed for the first time that afternoon. They passed from the hot sunshine outside to the dim coolness within, feeling a sensation of relief. Now they were able to breathe again. When a team is a team, you feel it most of all in the clubhouse. It was a different atmosphere and a different crowd of ballplayers from the struggling fourth-place Dodgers of July and August.

After a session with the Doc, who shook his head as he looked at the swelling elbow and insisted on treating it with cold compresses, Highpockets finally got away. Shedding his clothes, he ambled over to the showers. Most of the boys were finished, and they greeted him with shouts.

"Hey, there, Cecil, how many is that for you? Thirty-eight homers or thirty-nine? Jocko says it's thirty-eight. Is that your thirty-eighth or thirty-ninth?"

"Boy, you sure took a-holt of that one. I knew it was gone; the moment you connected I knew it was in there."

"Why, you old son-of-a-gun, look at that elbow! Doncha know better than to stop one of Jack Fuller's fast ones with yer elbow? Look at it, guys!"

"Hey, fellas, look at Highpockets' elbow. It's as big as a baseball!"

Then suddenly someone slapped him with the wet end of a towel. In six long months with the Dodgers it had never happened to him before.

He turned quickly, but the player had escaped to the other end of the room. Just then someone else slapped him with another wet towel. The blow stung his thigh. It also warmed his heart.

Slowly he went into the shower and returned to

his locker, sitting there happy and content despite that angry throbbing in his elbow, which was getting worse. As he yanked on his trousers, an attendant came past.

"Mr. McDade, they's a boy by the name of Kennedy outside. Says he's waiting for you. The kid just won't leave. Shall we send him home or what?"

"No, no, bring him in. Bring him in here, Steve."

A few minutes later Dean Kennedy entered, dressed in his best clothes, wide-eyed, silent and rather subdued by the strangeness of the scene. He stood watching the unfamiliar ballplayers while Highpockets finished dressing. In the boy's hand was a brand new league baseball.

"Like to have the gang sign that-there ball for you, Dean?" Highpockets extended his hand. A stab of pain went through his elbow as he took the ball.

"Gee, thanks. Thanks lots, Mr. McDade." Highpockets uncoiled himself from the bench and, taking Dean's fountain pen, went from one player to another with the ball. Finally it was covered with autographs. He returned to the bench where the boy was standing solemnly, watching. Under the youngster's arm was a folded newspaper which dropped to the floor as he reached out eagerly for the autographed baseball. It was a copy of the *Sporting News.*

Chapter 19

THE next day after the game, Highpockets sat on the rubbing table stripped to the waist while the Doc worked with concentration on the sore elbow, a worried look on his face. There was a pad around the elbow with several straps of surgeon's plaster holding it. Lester Young moved past just as the Doc was finishing.

"How's the old flipper, Cecil?"

"O.K., I reckon, Lester. O.K., thanks."

"Now you watch yerself, laddie. We need you out there," remarked the big first baseman, moving along. Several sportswriters sauntered up, and Highpockets greeted them as he slipped from the table.

"Why, hello, Tommy. Hello there, Casey, how are ya?"

Casey glanced quickly at his colleagues, who returned the look. "Why, thanks, Highpockets, I'm all right for an old guy. How are *you*? Think that elbow will straighten out before Jimmie Duveen and the Cards hit town, Doc?"

The Doc grunted. The grunt said anything at all you wished it to say. It said nothing whatever about the condition of the ailing arm or the team or the club's chances in those last few days of the season. Or it could mean a whole column starting like this:

"Doc Moran, the able and indefatigable trainer of the Brooklyn Dodgers, thinks his boys look better every day for the pennant . . ." And so forth for a thousand words.

"What's that thing? What ya got on that-there arm of his, Doc?" asked Tommy Revere of the *Times*.

"Epsom salt pad," said the Doc, always brief of speech, and more than usually curt with the reporters, whom he tolerated but did not cherish. He slapped Highpockets affectionately on the shoulder, the left shoulder. "Now, my boy, watch yourself tonight. Change it at least twice, remember; oftener if it gets dry. Razzle! Come here! Lemme have a look at your ankle."

Highpockets slipped from the table and went over to his locker, followed by the two sportswriters. Bob Russell reached up from his bench and caught at him as he passed.

"Hey, Cecil, hey there. What's he say about yer arm?"

"Coming round O.K., thanks, Bob."

They reached his locker and Casey remarked casually, "Just how did it happen, Highpockets?"

"Why, it was a slider that broke in on me. I tried to duck. I turned and got it full on the point of the elbow. Hurt? You bet it did! Thought I could shake it off, but the arm swelled fast and was pretty darn painful last night."

"Can you bat? That handicapped your batting today, didn't it?"

"I can hit O.K., but throwing, that's something else. Lucky I didn't have to throw. That might have hurt more than swinging a bat. But if the Cards think I can't throw, just let 'em try when they come in. I may fool 'em a little."

"Say, Highpockets, the crowd sure gave you a raspberry out there today. They wanted a hit the worst way your last time at bat. They hated to see you sacrifice."

He sat down and began yanking at his sock with one hand. "Shucks, I never feel at home here in Brooklyn less'n the crowd gives me a nice fat boo. Kinda peps me up, kinda."

"I figgered you'd go all out for a hit. I thought you'd want to preserve that record. I thought you'd try to meet the ball your last time up, Highpockets."

Before he could reply, Sandy Dockler of the *Telegram* joined them, one arm on Casey's shoulder, as he remarked: "Hey, there, Highpockets, how you feel about breaking your hitting streak? What you think about going hitless today?"

Highpockets leaned toward the locker, using his left arm and taking his shirt off a hook. There was an annoyed tone in his voice. "Think! I don't think anything, one way or another. We won the game, didn't we?"

"Yeah, sure. Only you had a chance for DiMag's record, didn't you know that?"

He drew his shirt on clumsily, favoring his right arm. "Look, boys, I'm not thinking 'bout records. I'm trying to play right field on a team. Last of the eighth, men on first and second, one run behind. They tell me to sacrifice. O.K. I sacrifice. What's records got to do with it? We won the game, didn't we? We're crawlin' up on them Cards, ain't we?"

There was a queer silence among the three sportswriters. And sportswriters are seldom at a loss for words.

"Oh," said Casey.

"Oh, yeah," said Dockler.

"Oh, I see," said Tommy Revere.

They looked at each other. They turned away.

That evening Highpockets was standing in the lobby of their hotel with Alan Whitehouse, short, swarthy, and the homeliest man on the club. A youngster edged up for an autograph. "Which one of you is Highpockets McDade?" he asked.

Raz Nugent, reading an evening paper a few feet away, saw the kid and heard his query. Instantly he stepped forward. "Why, now, I'm Highpockets," he said, taking the paper and signing for the boy. As the official jokester for the squad, Raz was overjoyed at the incident, and went round telling everyone how Alan, the homeliest man in Brooklyn, had been taken for Highpockets McDade.

An hour later Highpockets decided to call it a night, and went upstairs in the elevator. He was amazed to have the boy address him as Mr. Whitehouse and ask for his autograph. During the next twenty-four hours it seemed as if everyone in the hotel and outside made the same mistake. Waitresses in the Coffee Shoppe, elevator starters, bellboys, attendants at the ballpark, vendors, and autograph hounds of all sorts kept insisting he was Alan Whitehouse and demanding his signature. He was exasperated after a while.

It wasn't until he reached the field that he discovered the truth. Sitting on the bench with Fat Stuff before the game, the oldster chuckled and laughed when he heard about the confusion.

"Why, sure now, Cecil, it's a gag, that's all. Jest one of Raz Nugent's silly jokes, sort of thing he's always doing. Didn't you catch on? I seen him round last night, slipping bellboys half a buck to ask you that question. Don't let it bother you none, son."

Highpockets flushed. He was annoyed and slightly ashamed he had fallen so completely for Razzle's trick. Then the annoyance vanished, and a feeling of warmth and gratitude came over him. Now he was one of them, for they only played gags on those they liked. At last he was a part of the team, not just a long-ball hitter out there slugging for himself.

"Shucks, Fat Stuff! I was a sap, wasn't I now? I shore was. Dunno, though, it's kinda nice at that. Makes a fella feel he's one of the boys. Y'know, I'm real glad I didn't see through that gag, I really am."

The old coach yanked at the brim of his cap, peering out across the sun-swept diamond. "Yeah, you're one of 'em now, all right. Some ballplayers, they jest never do get to be one of the gang. Seems like they ain't team players nor ever will be. Then they wonder why they end up in Elmira or Duluth. You, now, you're out there risking that throwing arm of yours 'cause you're one of 'em. You don't hesitate. You go out and take chances for the team. Say, don't think the boys aren't wise, either. They know what that doc told you. Yes, sir, you bet they do." He spat into the dirt before the dugout. "That's the trouble with this country nowadays, everyone out for himself, aiming to hit the long ball over the fence."

Spike Russell came tramping in. He spoke in a crisp voice that had overtones of fatigue in it.

"Alan! Take over Cecil's spot in right. Cecil, you'll rest up this afternoon."

Highpockets rose instantly. He grabbed his glove. His face was angry. "Spike, I want to go in there."

The manager laid a hand on the tall boy's arm. "Doctor's orders, kid, doctor's orders. He's seen those X-rays, and what he saw ain't good. Besides, we need you for the Cards on Saturday worse'n we do for the Phils today. Take it easy, Cecil, you've sure earned a day off for yourself."

So Highpockets watched that game from the coolness of the bench. At the end of the afternoon, the Dodgers were only a game back of the Cards, the closest they had been all season.

That evening he spent with Dean Kennedy. Highpockets' elbow was stiff and he could hardly bend his arm, so he used his left hand as the two of them leaned over the stamp album. On the dining room table was a bowl of water, filled with bits of colored paper. Near it lay the tweezers, the water-mark detector, the perforation gauge, the stamp hinges spilled everywhere, the catalogue turned to Hong Kong. They worked for over an hour, their talk about the stamps often interrupted by questions from the boy about the coming series with the Cards, or requests for baseball information that Highpockets was not always able to supply.

"One dollar on ninety-six cents, violet red. That's sure a dilly, isn't it, Mr. McDade? Yep, a nice specimen. I traded that with George Mason last week. He's a great swopper, George is. Lemme see now, that must be number forty-three, 1891, don't you guess? Say, Mr. McDade." He straightened up and leaned back in his chair. "Tell me something. This man Glen Harrison, d'you think he'll ever make the grade in the big leagues?"

"Hold on, Dean. I'm not as certain as you about that stamp. It might mebbe be number fifty-three, one dollar on ninety-six cents *black*, not violet red. That would make it 1893, no, '98, not '91. See? That's where it fits in, there. How's that now? Harrison? You mean Glen Harrison? Why, I really wouldn't know; I wouldn't know about him. I played with his brother Jack in Mobile, but I never knew Glen. He's an all right sort of ballplayer, I'd say, a pretty fair pitcher . . ."

"Aw, Mr. McDade!" The boy looked at him and there was disappointment in his tones. "He's not a pitcher! He's a first baseman; played last year with the Knoxville Smokies in the Tri-State League." He paused a second for breath and then continued faster than ever. "An' . . . an' . . . an' he batted .298 an' fielded .985 an' this year he's gone to Savannah in the South Atlantic League an' hit fourteen homers an' they say Dave Leonard of the Browns has his eye on him, an' . . . an' . . . an' . . ."

"Hey, wait a minute. Hold on there. Wait a minute, Dean. Look, where on earth d'you get all this from?"

"That's right," he almost shouted. "I know it's right. It's true, Mr. McDade. He was with Knoxville, an' now he's hitting .304 fer Savannah, an' . . . an' . . . an' . . ."

"Yeah, shore, I know hit's right. Only where d'you get it all from? Hey?" His eye fell upon a pile of magazines, stamp magazines that were heaped on the side table. On top of the magazines was the latest copy of the *Sporting News*.

"Oh . . . I d'know." Dean subsided. "I jest read about him."

Highpockets shook his head. For a kid who didn't care for baseball when the Dodgers were skidding into fifth place back in July, he was certainly doing all right. He rose. Well, that's what baseball is; if it gets you, it gets you hard.

"I must be movin'."

"Aw, no! We have lots more to do tonight. We haven't done the Western Australias yet."

"Not tonight. It's past yer bedtime, and mine,

too. Besides, this old elbow is acting up. I must put it to soak. Now look, Dean. Here's yer ticket for tomorrow. It's raining now. Effen this keeps up all day and there is no game, this ticket is not good for the next day. See? I'll hafta grab you off another. But don't lose it. An' be shore when you get into the park to keep the stub, 'cause should the game be called before four and a half innings, that stub will admit you to the postponed game. Understand? Careful with it now; better put this away in your purse."

The boy fished from his hip pocket a grimy and well-worn wallet, stuffed with papers. He took the ticket, fingered it fondly for a minute, mumbled a thank-you, and tried to jam it into a compartment of the overcrowded purse. As he did so, a small, oblong card was visible on top of the pack of papers.

Highpockets glanced at it. It was the photo of a player at bat, lunging for the ball. There was a familiar look to that swing. Underneath the picture the caption read:

CECIL "HIGHPOCKETS" McDADE
Right Field, Brooklyn, N.L.

Chapter 20

At last, at the tail end of the season, after weeks and weeks of discouragement and disappointment in fourth place and fifth place, the Dodgers had caught the Cards. They were even at last. Needing only a victory on the second day of the series to go ahead, every fan in Brooklyn and every member of the club realized in those final moments of the pennant race that once ahead, they would never be overhauled.

The Brooks sat on the bench watching the Cards at practice, trying to pretend it was just another ballgame, all of them knowing in their hearts it wasn't. That this was it! This was the big day, the game they had been pointing for all season and even before, ever since those brisk, windy mornings in the Florida spring when everyone was fresh and loose and keen. Now they were tight; tired, too, and there were lines around their eyes and mouths showing nobody had slept well the previous night. They betrayed their nervousness as they sat chew-

174

ing vigorously, talking with sportswriters who stood before the dugout. Everyone was pretending it didn't matter, like a man about to have his tooth pulled. Actually they all knew this was it.

Highpockets held his arm stiffly, in an awkward position, and you could see it was painful. There was a bump plainly visible on the right elbow, a swelling that wouldn't go down despite the Epsom salt pads and the electric blanket on it all night long. Suppose what the specialist said was true! Suppose he injured his arm for good if he went on using it! What then? As the boys like to say, a ball player with a bum arm is just a groundskeeper with a glove on. Ask Sonny Jones, who used to be with the Red Sox, Highpockets was thinking. He's a pinch hitter and utility outfielder for Wenatchee now. Ask old Hank Kraus, formerly of the Indians. He's a scout for K. C. Or George McMurry, who won twenty-two for the Cubs, now tending a gas station in Depaw, South Carolina. If you can't throw, your usefulness in baseball is over.

Someone asked whether it hurt. Silly question. You only had to look at his face to see. But he replied politely and quietly, too. "It's my hand now. Seems like my whole hand hurts. Gee, I shore hated to leave that game yesterday, but my elbow began to swell up on me, and I knew I was no use to the gang. I just couldn't throw. Boy, you have to be able to throw against them Cards. They got speed; they run everything out; they don't concede a thing. So I had to quit in the seventh. But I shore hated to, I shore did."

"Will you start this afternoon, Highpockets?"

"Start? 'Course I'll start. I'll be in there all right."

"Hey, Highpockets, the doc thinks you shouldn't. He told Spike Russell if you do, your arm may go. If you begin throwing out there today, he said he wouldn't be responsible. He said you might ruin it for good and all."

"Shucks, that sawbones! I'll throw all right, I'll be in there throwing at the end."

They looked at him and said nothing. Funny chap, this Highpockets McDade from a North Carolina farm. Supposed to be only interested in himself and his batting average, his home-run record. Yet here he is, risking his arm and his future as a ballplayer on this one game. Funny sort of chap, hard to dope out.

The team went out to practice with Paul Roth in right. The fans wondered. Then the boys came back to the bench and sat round waiting for the bell. Down in the dugout, Jocko Klein was putting the tools on and talking in his serious way about Jimmie Duveen of the Cards. The big Redbird hurler was warming up over across the way.

"Glad I don't have to catch that guy. He hides

the ball behind his glove, throws his foot up in your face, looks over at a blonde behind first base, and bang! It's past before you can see the darn thing."

"Right, Jocko," spoke up Bob Russell. "You can't hit what you don't see. Holy catfish! He's plenty bad in the daytime, but at night he's murder in the first degree. Thank heaven we ain't playing this game under the lights. Why, he can thread a needle with that-there fast ball of his'n."

Now the three Dodger relief men were off, carrying their gloves and their jackets under their arms, out to the bullpen in deep right. The bullpen was going into action from the start, for Spike was taking no chances. He wanted to be ready if young Chris Terry showed the least signs of wear and tear. The umpires were strolling up to the plate, where Charlie Draper met them with the batting list in his hand. As usual, the loudspeaker began on the line-ups, the fans listening with more than usual attention, wondering.

Is Paul Roth going in? Will Roth take over right in place of Highpockets? Who's playing the right garden? What's cooking? They had seen High-pockets taken out of the game the previous afternoon, and those who had not seen had read all about it. Every sporting column in the city was filled with medical terminology and news of his injury. Every sportswriter overnight became an expert on orthopedics.

"For Brooklyn. Young, numbah thirty, first base. Tucker, numbah thirty-four . . ." A great cheer rose across the diamond, echoing back and forth from the stands in deep center to the crowded tiers back of the plate, breaking in waves upstairs. Finally it died away.

"Swanson, numbah twelve, left field." Again that tremendous burst of noise for the old favorite, a torrent of sound that completely drowned out the announcer's next words. The old man is taking over left. Spike sure needs this game; he's working every angle. What about the clean-up spot? Will Highpockets go in? How about Highpockets? Is Roth taking over right or will Highpockets play today?

The announcer was forced to repeat the next sentence because no one heard it. He did so, clearly and with emphasis.

"And in right field . . ."

There was a pause, a long pause. He knew there was drama in his words, and he hung over them. Silence settled on the ballpark, a silence so intense you could hear the telegraph instruments ticking furiously away in the press box above the grandstand. No one moved; no one spoke. The umpires stood motionless by the plate. Still the announcer hesitated.

Highpockets! How 'bout Highpockets? Is he gonna play or ain't he? Is Paul Roth going in for Highpockets?

"And in right field . . . McDade . . . numbah . . ."

It was the roll and roar of the sea. It was a hundred planes together in the sky. It was a spontaneous and sudden tumult which enveloped the field and everyone in it, every man, woman, and child. There were no hoots, no moans, no groans or angry jeers. No raucous calls across the diamond.

This time it was different. It was different because the fans in the bleachers can't well be fooled. The boys in the ninety-cent seats know baseball better than anyone. They also know something else—they know human values. They recognize a player who is only interested in how many base knocks he gets. They recognize the phony more quickly from the bleachers than from anywhere else; the bleachers are a good place from which to see baseball and the individuals who make it up. The fans there are also quick to recognize the right guy, the team player.

So they yelled and yelled. At last Highpockets belonged to Brooklyn.

Chapter 21

THERE are almost three million people in Brooklyn, and only thirty-five thousand that day had succeeded in getting past the cordon of policemen set up early in the morning on the streets around Ebbets Field. Unless you could show a ticket, you couldn't approach the place. The rest of the population got the game in other ways. No work was done throughout the city. In offices telephones rang unanswered while the clerks gathered around a radio, listening intently, saying nothing as inning after inning went by. Where there were no radios handy, a boy was sent downstairs to keep bulletins flowing from the nearest grill. Usually the boy had only to go as far as the elevator. As the afternoon grew older, every elevator man and every starter knew the exact score. Each person who entered the building asked the same question or made the same remark. "Still nothing to nothing?" "Yes, still no score yet."

In the taverns all over town, in Manhattan and the Bronx, and of course, in Queens, crowds hung

around the television sets, watched Spike Russell
have a field day at short, saw Highpockets' tight
face when he came up to bat, and big Jim Duveen,
pitching the game of his life, mow down the Brooklyn sluggers. On the streets, strangers spoke to
strangers as they never do in New York, and everyone asked the same thing. "Anybody scored yet?"
All afternoon white-coated soda jerkers came out
of corner drugstores and posted up goose eggs on
the sheet stuck to the front window pane. Folks
sat in taxis long after they had paid the bill, because for once drivers were content to sit and listen, too, and manage the Dodgers for a change.
Around the parked cars by the curb, little knots
of people bent forward in silence, nodding as the
Brooks pulled themselves out of hole after hole,
inning after inning. Truck drivers even made peace
with their enemies, the traffic cops, hurling the
latest score at them as they turned into the main
avenues of town.

Shadows deepened over the tall buildings of the
city, while out on the diamond in Brooklyn the two
teams battled on, neither one giving way. It was
hot, cruelly hot, one of those steaming July days
which get misplaced into the end of September,
which descend upon a metropolis already old and
weary from the summer heat. No one minded the

heat that afternoon. Everyone was thinking of the game.

It was Duveen's day. He was a money player and this was the game to win, the last chance, the one the Cards needed most of all. He was determined to get it. His fast ball was smoke, his curve broke angrily, his side-arm sinker fooled the batters. He slaughtered the top of the order, forcing them to pop up, to fly out, or to hit lazy grounders to the infield. It was Duveen's day, all right, but not Chris Terry's. The young Dodger was in trouble from the start. Only expert fielding saved him from a score more than once, as the Cards went to work on him in those early innings.

Spike Russell was the take-charge guy all over the infield. He played shortstop; he played third base; he went out to smother tricky Texas leaguers that the aged Swanny never in the world could have reached; he roamed far to his right to turn hits into double-play balls; he raced to the stands in short left for fouls that would have been impossible for most men and got them. In the second, in the fourth, in the fifth and sixth, the Cards had men on bases and Chris on the ropes. He was saved in each inning by brilliant work in the field.

In the eighth it seemed that the game was over. From deep right, Highpockets was a spectator to the drama. Up to then he had caught a couple of routine flies but had never been forced to throw. The first man singled and reached the pick-off post as Chris weakened again and gave a base on balls. First and second were occupied when Spike signaled to the bullpen. The youngster walked dejectedly off the mound, the crowd applauded, and Bones Hathaway came in from right. No one down and the top of the Card batting order at the plate.

Anxious to give the batter nothing to hit, Bones lost the first man he faced and the bags were loaded. Every player and every fan in the park realized that a single tally might win the game. Highpockets thumped his glove nervously with his fist. As he did so, pain shot up and down his sore arm. Bonesey went carefully to work on the batter, who stood fouling pitch after pitch to the screen behind. Finally he lifted a fly back of first, which Lester smothered while the runners held. There was dynamite in the air as Steve Carone, the Card clean-up man, stepped in.

They were off on the next pitch, all three. The batter hit a stinging grounder to the right of second, a single seemingly through the hole into center. Bob Russell went for it with one of his leaping stabs. He stopped it, reaching out with one hand, and in the same motion tossed to Spike on second.

Now the third-base runner was nearing home

plate, and only a double-play could prevent that vital score. Spike's bare hand speared the ball and, touching the base, he jumped high to avoid the spikes of the sliding runner. He whirled as he leaped and came down to burn the ball to Lester at first. Lester's glove stretched for it and the umpire's hand went up. The batter was out by a step, the tally didn't count, and another zero flashed upon the scoreboard in deep right field.

Bonesey kept the Cards off the bases until the twelfth, when they started to go again. Mike Madden, the Redleg first baseman, fast and powerful, singled to Roy in center. The next hitter smacked a line drive over third and the Card coaches yelled, "Go for two, Mike, go for two!" With a burst of speed he slid safely into third, so there were two aboard once more with no one down.

Bonesey went to work, struck out the catcher, and started on the tail end of the batting list with confidence. The next man caught one of his sliders and laced it to right. Highpockets knew the Cards would take a chance on his sore arm at the first opportunity. This was it.

A great sigh, a collective "Oh" from the crowd went up as the ball was hit. Then he came charging over fast and it slapped into his glove with a smack you could hear from one end of the tense ballpark to the other. Highpockets turned without hesitation as the runner on third sprinted for home.

Two hundred and eighty feet from right field to the plate, a fast man on the bases, a race between ball and man. Highpockets drew back and let go. It was a deadline peg, a perfect strike into Jocko's glove, slightly to the third base side of the plate where he needed it to block off the burly Card trying to slide in under him. Hold that ball, Jocko, hold that ball, kid!

Jocko held it. The runner was out, the score shut off, and the Cards were racing out for the last of the thirteenth, muttering to themselves about that sore arm of McDade's which wasn't supposed to last out the series.

For fifteen long innings Duveen pitched shut-out ball and there was no score on either side. In the sixteenth St. Louis finally got a man on third and squeezed home that important run, the first of the game. The Dodgers came to bat in an uproar that became a frenzy, after Lester had flied out, when Roy Tucker drove a pitch cleanly over second. Swanny sacrificed him to second base, so there were two down as Highpockets stepped in. Every spectator and all the millions outside the park listening in had the same thought.

A homer would win the game. Over the fence

into Bedford Avenue, one of Highpockets' favorite shots, and bang, the contest would be finished.

The Cards knew this, too. Would they pitch to him? Highpockets had gone hitless all afternoon, and Jocko, next at bat, was hitting .340 and had made three of the Dodgers' six hits that day. Would they pass Highpockets and take a chance on Jocko?

They chose to pitch to him and Duveen went to work calmly, giving him those close-to-the-handle balls. But the hurler failed to realize that he had changed his batting stance. His left foot was ten inches behind his normal position, so he was squared away and ready to hit a good one to left. Actually it was a change-of-pace ball that he hit, a liner down the left field foul line, about ten feet in, right in the slot where they least expected it. Roy was lightning on the bases, cutting over third by the time the left fielder reached the ball and across with the tying run before Highpockets slid into third with a triple.

He was stranded when the Cardinal center fielder hauled down Jocko's hard-hit drive close to the fence. Now the score was tied, and the contest continued. In the seventeenth, with a man on base, Alan Whitehouse went in as a pinch hitter for Bonesey, and in the eighteenth, Jerry Fielding, the third hurler for the Brooks, took over the pitching assignment. Still Duveen kept going for the Cards.

No score in the eighteenth. In the first of the nine-teenth the Redlegs went down in order. With no one out in the last half, Highpockets came to bat again. The memory of that game-saving triple was in the minds of the crowd and they howled for a home-run punch to win. Into the formation on the right went the Cards, and back against the fence went the three outfielders, each one glancing nerv-ously over his shoulder at the wall behind. It was the big moment of the long afternoon, for now they were afraid of him, every one of them.

"Make him pitch to you, make him pitch to you, Cecil," shouted Draper back of third base.

Highpockets had his orders. Selecting the ball, he took a wicked cut and laced a liner directly at the spot where the shortstop would normally have been playing. It was so plainly aimed at open terri-tory that the crowd rose cheering, yelling and shrieking as he rounded first and then cut back to the bag. For the first time that afternoon the Car-dinal bullpen went to work furiously.

Still Duveen was not through. He rose to the occasion as he had so many times, and choked off the rally and the roar of the crowd simultaneously. That roar, from every portion of the stands, died suddenly as Jocko hit a deep fly which the St. Louis center fielder caught and Spike, trying desper-ately to advance Highpockets, hit a pop-up which the pitcher nabbed between the mound and first base. So the winning run was still on first with two men out.

Bob Russell strolled up to face the tired hurler, who seemed to be getting out of this jam as he had been doing all afternoon. The noise died off; the fans couldn't take it any more. They felt that the game would go on forever. They could have turned on the lights and played all night without another score, so well was Duveen pitching, so evenly were the two teams matched.

The break came when it was least expected. Bob fouled off a couple of pitches upstairs, and then smashed a wicked line drive just inside first base. The first baseman stabbed for it and missed, and the ball rolled out into foul ground in deep right. Highpockets' long legs ate up the ground as he raced for third. By this time the relay was coming in to the second baseman, who stood with his back to the plate out on the grass toward right field.

Charlie Draper sized up the situation at a glance. There was a chance—the unexpected, the daring play, a tired man in the field, a speedster on the basepaths. It might work. He gave Highpockets the green light and Highpockets went. Rounding third without hesitation, he wheeled and raced for home.

The second baseman turned, saw Highpockets

pass third on his way to the plate, and started at the sight. A quick and accurate throw would have cut him down easily with feet to spare. But the fielder had to recover from that momentary shock of surprise. He drew back and let go hurriedly. The throw was short. The Card catcher had to take several steps forward for the ball, and Highpockets slid in safely through a monsoon of dust.

Confusion! Noise! The crowd on its feet, shrieking. Up above, the organ playing, "Leave Us Go Watch The Dodgers, Rogers." The whole team is out at the plate, surrounding Highpockets as he rises from the dirt. Here comes Spike rushing from the dugout. He grabs off the big fellow's cap and ruffles up his hair. He pounds him on the back. He jams the cap back on his head once more.

There goes Highpockets toward the dugout! Now he's tipping his cap—to a kid frantically waving a scorecard at him from the front box over the Dodger dugout.